Anna,

THE DALI SQUIGGLE

A NOVELLA

NICK SWEENEY

Some more words for you. Nick

All rights reserved, no part of this publication may be reproduced or transmitted by any means whatsoever without the prior permission of the publisher.

Text © Nick Sweeney
Cover photo © Nick Sweeney
any additional images are sourced from the public domain

Edited by Julia Krzyzanowska Cover image modified by Veneficia Publications.

ISBN: 978-1-916756-16-8
Veneficia Publications
February 2024
VENEFICIA PUBLICATIONS UK
veneficiapublications.com

To my friend in Spain

CONTENTS

ONE 1

TWO 21

THREE 74

FOUR 160

FIVE 182

ONE

The town is planned for romance, all those vistas – no other word for them – all those buildings in between them. They become the backdrop of your romance. What if you live in an ugly village, though? Where's your backdrop, and what's in it? What, trees? Then there is no romance, only relationships. And because there is no romance, those relationships have a good chance of breaking down. On the bright side, though, there will be no sadness at the vista, at the buildings, no regretful thoughts of how you once walked there, and experienced romance.

There is romance on the Metro: an office chair left on a Metro train, an opportunity for a couple in love to amuse each other and charm strangers around them, leave an impression of the romance of the city. At North Shields, though? Sort of. Paris would be better, though, or Berlin, Budapest perhaps. Madrid might do too.

If you live in a village, you can saunter along the street to see your love. You can do it at the last minute, in your stay-home clothes that stink. You don't do that in a town. You need to plan; you need to sort out your route – the trains, or the buses – the Metro – or parking, you have to take the time to anticipate. It's the difference between phoning up a talk radio station to make a comment or going on a TV show to do so; one is the real truth, spur-of-the-moment, with your icky teeth and in your stained pyjamas, and the other is all artifice, making an impression that is extra-curricular and, to be honest, off-topic, in your fancy clothes and bright grin and the hope that your mam will tape it. Romance needs its parties to make an impression.

When the strings swirl with city lovers' hearts, there is a fine backdrop of old and venerable buildings to echo them. This won't happen in the village square, or in the car park of its only pub. You can pass them any time. Who cares what memories are left in places like that?

After a month in Madrid, Alex Dante felt like a *Madrileño*, landlocked and far from the sea, sun and sky that usually conjured up the idea of Spain. It had taken just as long for Alex to see that teaching English to Spaniards was not for him. He hated the whiff of children's unwashed hair when he bent to check their work and hated the thick sense of agitation from the hormones leaking from teen pores. And adults didn't go to language schools because they were serious about learning a language; they wanted to make friends, or better still, meet the love of their life. Alex decided not to stand in their way with his stupid lesson plans. He reverted to what he thought of as his default career, behind a bar.

During his degree at Newcastle, he had often felt that his most successful venture on the trudge towards his two-two had been his part-time bar work in the Hedgehog, an off-city-centre pub. Bored while livening up his CV with his Urban Planning BA, he had frivolously added the abbreviations BD, for Bishop Desmond Tutu, and BM, for barman. He noticed to his horror that he had forgotten to remove them before sending it off to accompany a hundred job applications. He had hoped to return to his native London to work, but there were complications in the shape of a radiant, retro-styled hairdresser called Eileen, who did not want to live among the people she referred to jokingly, at least sometimes, as *soft southern bastards*. Fair enough, but Alex had felt torn. The Tyne Tees Town Planning Department had ignored his rogue abbreviations and come to his rescue with a job helping to adjudicate on the placement of street furniture. Dreary meetings led to notifications generating storms of correspondence, demonstrations and lawsuits, from transport officials, small businessmen, decidedly non-small businessmen with great sweary voices and great hairy fists, shouty pressure groups and apoplectic motorists.

Alex had been living with Eileen for three months before it became clear that one of them was controlling, petty and scary. He had sometimes been successfully gaslighted into thinking it was him. It took them a few months to extricate themselves from their relationship and its toxic labyrinth of a flat, utility bills, loans, possessions and friends.

With the expenses of life minus Eileen's income and driven out too by his solitude – the friends had unsurprisingly rallied around Eileen – Alex supplemented his day job by returning to work a few evenings at the Hedgehog. He liked the simplicity of it: people wanted a drink, and for an agreed price, he gave it to them. They did not discuss the issues around it – well, the odd mentalist did – nor did they attend meetings about it... well, not until they enrolled in AA, but that was a long way along from Alex's part in their fate.

He could not jack in his career as a thorn-in-the-side of urban interest groups to do full-time bar work though. Could he? His dad had been an old-school shirt-and-tie barman, a relic from the days when bar work wasn't just what students and Australians did till they found a proper job. Jeffrey Dante had carried a whiff of his trade on him – beer and tobacco and wood polish – and had taken pride in his work, but he had been anxious for Alex to do something better.

One slow night at work, Alex was half-listening to a customer home on a break from teaching English in Poland. As she held court with the friends she had left behind, it was clear that she was disdainful of people who went off to teach in places like Spain – Eastern Europe was *the* place, she asserted. Several, in fact, thought Alex the pedant, but he kept the remark to himself. He also thought that if you were in Newcastle, you really would not want to go anywhere colder. One aspect of life as a TEFLer intrigued Alex: it seemed that you could answer an ad on

Monday, have an interview on Wednesday, fly on Saturday, and be living a different life in a different country by the following Monday. That had a cool ring to it that never quite let him escape it.

⁓

Lesson 1, Unit 1

What is your name? Possible answers:
My name is...
I am...
Who wants to know?

What is your friend's name? Possible answers:
His name is...
He is...
Alas, I have no friends.

What is the essential misery at the heart of your existence that brings you to my class?
Answer freely and continue on a separate sheet if necessary. Or a blanket.

Alex would not have minded a different life. Newcastle was like a foreign country to him anyway. And it was hard to love either of his jobs, with two sets of colleagues to be irritated by. Perhaps it was time to find a proper foreign country? It was definitely time to find another girl. He was twenty-five, and loneliness did not suit him. He had always liked the Mediterranean look; a señorita could be perfect.

On his degree, there had been a funding requirement for students to cram an EU language. He had chosen Spanish. Back in school he had not been good at French, and he did not like the way German sounded. Spanish was difficult but, sometimes, almost enjoyable.

He had been to Spain once, accompanied his dad to Mojacar on the south-east coast. In response to a family emergency in Ireland, Alex's mum had dropped out of the holiday. Alex had somewhat reluctantly gone in her place, and yet it had been the best thing to happen to him. He had not spoken to his dad properly since embarking on his tediously rebellious teenage years, so catching up had been intriguing. Alex had fond memories of Mojacar: the sight of his dad free of cares, their frequency of the English bars there and his dad's sometimes embarrassing assertions that they could do with somebody to show them how it was really done. His dad had succumbed to renal cancer within a year.

Perhaps Alex had the coast in mind when he fixed on deserting his stuttering teaching career and Madrid's Cambridge College, whose sole Cambridge connection was that one of the school owners – three women called Marguerita – had taken a day trip there years before. The fact that it was January had given him pause. A town like Mojacar, he assumed, closed down in November and opened again in April. He was sketching out his vague plan to his colleague Math, who reminded him that there were a thousand bars in Madrid.

"Can you speak Spanish, though, mate?" Math wondered.

About to say no, Alex realised that he could, a bit. His meagre social life had been passed among his fellow-teachers, but he negotiated his shopping in Spanish, bought bus tickets, had his hair cut and, just once, mercifully, got through a root canal filling – the receptionist lied when she said the dentist spoke English.

"Of course I can," he told Math and he nodded, smiled on the outside and panicked inside as he wondered if he really could.

≷

"Were those beers in the fridge yours?"
"Yes."
"We wondered whose they were."
"Yes?"
"Yes. If they kind of belonged to anybody, you know? We wondered."
"Then you drank them."
"Yes – soz."
"That green mould on the saucer is also mine."
"Yes? Oh. Okay. Thought so."
"You didn't eat it, though."
"No."

The school's director of studies had been pissed off with him. They had paid his airfare, he reminded Alex, sorted his accommodation and launched his new career. Alex had raised his eyebrows at the last part then calmly negotiated two weeks' notice. He agreed to pay half the airfare back; if the idiot director really wanted to get into the micro-economics of it, Alex had been their minion for nearly four months, a chunk of his life in exchange for a one-way on Easyjet. He would not miss the run-down apartment in Las Rozas, a share with two guys whose hygiene, kitchen habits and haphazard approach to personal space and property had left much to be desired. He promised to vacate the place the day after he finished teaching.

His plan was to flop in a cheap hotel and spend his waking hours trying to nail a bar job. If he failed and ran out of money, he would go home, stay at his mum's, work in a local boozer for a while. Or find another town to mess up with badly-thought-out planning. Or do more TEFL, possibly in Poland.

I am Dante. Dante.
Not the Dante. A Dante.
Do you see the difference?

You can stay over.
To make a negative example: you can not stay over.

You can use the guest toothbrush.
You can use a guest toothbrush.
Which of these is the best option?

People sometimes asked Alex if he was Italian – at least educated people who had heard of Dante Alighieri did. Alex finally had to give in and take their word that Dante had been as great a poet as they said. Despite his occasional spurts of reading, he could not get to grips with Dante's works. It was not his fault, he decided nor, he allowed, Dante's, who probably just worked best in medieval Italian.

If Alex was in the mood, he told the story of his surname. His great-great-great-grandfather, emancipated from slavery in the southern states of America, refused to bear the surname of his former master. Being a *reading man* – or a pretentious one, Alex's dad suggested – he had named himself after the author of the one thing he had taken from the slaver's house, a copy of Dante's *Inferno*.

"Lucky he didn't nick an ironing board," Alex's dad was fond of saying. Then Alex's great grandfather, following a life as a sailor, brought the name to Trinidad. Alex's granddad Carlton had imported it to England.

The first person to ask Alex, "Dante – what, like the poet?" was a secondary school history teacher. Alex came home and asked his dad, "Why didn't you tell me Dante was the name of a poet?"

"Of *course* it is." Jeffrey had laughed. "Don't ask me which one, though."

"Well, it was – *honestly*, Dad..." Alex had unconsciously adopted a new gravity, sometimes charming, sometimes annoying, since starting secondary school. "It was *Dante*, of course," he spluttered.

"Oh yeah?" Jeffrey Dante was a wind-up artist; his job behind the bar, his contact with both wise men and fools, imbued him with a wit that was sometimes erudite, sometimes crude, but always quick. His eyes sparkled as he rummaged in the bookcase, pulled out a copy of the *Inferno*, blew some dust off of it a little ceremoniously, and therefore facetiously, and handed it to Alex, wishing him luck with it.

Alex had swept uncurious eyes over it before, he remembered. It was not the copy liberated more than a century before from a slave exploiter's mansion, but an edition Carlton had bought in the nineteen forties. Even so, with its covers etched in gold leaf and its marbled endpapers, it was a breath of antiquity: a thing of proper beauty.

Jeffrey Dante did not appreciate the delicate arts of rhyme in any language. He drummed the importance of education into Alex at any opportunity, something practical, the path to a job that was not behind a bar. Though neither of them could know that it was Alex's destiny to tend a bar, he was immune to poetry anyway.

"You don't *look* Italian," some people told Alex. He had to work out from the nuances whether they were being genuinely cosmopolitan or disingenuously racist. Others said, "I *knew* you were Italian."

"My mum's Irish," Alex's story continued, if he wanted it to. "I don't look Irish, either."

"Ah, you do *so*, now," one Irish wit had said.

The other oddity in the naming of Alex Dante was that he was simply Alex, not Alexander. He sometimes hankered after being an Alexander – the regality of it, the history – except when he had to write his name out. He appreciated his short name's snappiness then.

One of the last things he did at the Cambridge College was to type those names at the head of a hasty CV update, some of it in his best Spanish. He printed one out and checked its lack of superfluous abbreviations. Realising that no bar manager would be arsed to read it, he screwed it up and whizzed it into a bin. He picked up some of the menus the teachers had collected, either for delivery orders or teaching aids and, as was their habit with almost anything, dropped as soon as they were finished with them, wherever they happened to be standing. He checked that they had translations and slipped them into his bag.

In Madrid there is a woman who bears a name I will like. Not just one – lots of women whose names I like, all those... Spanish names. As the old song nearly says, and ought (if I may make so bold) to say, hallo and greetings, you fair Spanish ladies, greetings and hallo, you fair ladies of Spain.

Alex had a parallel CV. The last entry on it was not Eileen, but a girl with the unappealing name of Mog, short for Imogen. That had lasted four of the five weeks of their TEFL course in Bilbao. He had never felt a true spark strike with her. And anyway, she had been set on Barcelona. He would fall in love in Madrid, he hoped, with a girl bearing a name he liked. Along with getting a job, that was his only plan. Both came true for him just a week after leaving the Cambridge College.

All Alex's brain-challenging affairs had been with dark-haired, petite, nervy women. The sex had always been frenzied and intense and had pushed almost everything else – plans, friends, decorum – into second place. Its intensity was sometimes matched later by paranoia and accusations, or simply a void that just could not be filled. He thought of avoiding such women – go for blowsy, busty blondes, perhaps – but then fell into the orbit of Maria Betancur at work at Madrid's biggest mixed gay bar, the Solano, and immediately abandoned the idea.

She was short and dark, with the kind of spare, bony body that Alex would worship if given the chance. She was wavy-haired, had big eyes holding a promise of amusement, was indeed funny, and kind. She dressed unflashily well, a little formal at times, and smelt subtly fragrant. Maria was exactly his type – she was the *one*, his optimism convinced him. He was young enough to be lovelorn, and, in some perverse way, to enjoy it. Maria knew that Alex loved her, the first time she found herself trapped in his over-frank gaze.

At the club, everybody is ecstatic on the outside. On the inside they are not, despite the ingestion of actual ecstasy. They are faced with their actual hopelessness. The music drowns out the voices inside that scream and accuse. The smiles and the nudges, the movements of the dance, edge the cares away. Not just the cares, death and relatives and money worries, but the nags: clear out the wet stuff under the sink, get that intermittently aching tooth seen to, the stain on that door is not going to go away of its own accord, and needs painting, and then you have to do the whole door, and then, probably, the frame, and then, quite possibly, the other doors. Curse that three-beat rest that allows such thoughts in, but then they are gone. For a while.

Alex and Maria were the only straights who worked in Solano. Stupidly, Alex had not realised that Solano was gay. It had simply been the first place to beckon him with a *staff wanted* sign in its window the morning after he jacked in the TEFL job. The manager, Juan Pereiro, may have assumed that Alex was gay. It was a habitual inference from the way he walked, how he wore his clothes and placed his hands as he held a book or a drink. There was also something in Alex's voice, a reticence that some people mistook for camp.

"But you've *been* gay, right?" two pushy guys had asked him, at different times and in different social circles, narked at their skew-whiff gaydar. Another once insisted, "You're gay, Alex – you just don't know it yet." Juan Pereiro, occupied in checking out Alex's Spanish and that he knew his food and drink – Alex's study of the menus had paid off – and ascertaining that he talked a good game on the subject of a busy bar, did not care.

Solano's story was that it was the happiest place in Madrid, but really it was just some bar. Some of the punters were constantly up, some down, but most were in between, like anywhere else. One regular signalled the end of his night by declaring loudly, "I don't know who I *am*," to anybody who would listen. Alex was alarmed the first time he saw the performance, then saw it was a ploy, and a rather crap one, to attract somebody who would be able to remind him who he was and take him home to do so.

"It's only a fucking *disco*," Alex was tempted to call if he was stressed and feeling nasty – pop the bubble – but the guy was just trying to prolong the Solano's illusion for as long as he willed it. And what was wrong with that? All bars needed that little something to get people into them and staying and spending. Nothing was wrong with it except that Alex was usually by then at the point of wanting his own night to end. When the Solano was in full swing, it didn't matter whether Alex was gay or straight, Irish or Italian, because he was too busy for anything other than work. In between transactions, he sent looks at Maria, tried to make them sophisticated and self-assured, but knew they were just boyish and moony.

He knew that, for a while at least, everything he said to Maria would be full of a meaning he wanted to put over and yet also wanted to hide. It would all sound like a line to get her knickers off and, true, he wanted to do that, but he also wanted all of her, in a way that sometimes mystified him. He had lucid moments when he could dismiss his infatuation with her and could deem himself free of it. In the mirror the next morning, though, he would catch a ridiculous look in his eye. He cursed but was happy and waited not just to make any old move on Maria, but to make the right one.

What was that song about a perfect day called? What would be a great title for a song about a perfect day? Whatever it was called, I will be glad I will have spent it with you. Risking my all, I am glad in advance that I will have spent it with you.

One time after the early shift, they caught the last weeknight Metro. Alex and Maria took turns to sit on an abandoned office chair. It wheeled gently back and forth with their weight as they put their arms out at first to steady themselves, then made a game of it, lifted their legs so as not to impede the momentum. Maria had looked exceptionally smart in a tweed jacket that was both pink and brown – terracotta, he supposed – and a knee-length black pleated skirt, dark stockings that covered her legs up to mid-thigh, and dinky oxblood loafers. Alex guessed that to their audience of late-night commuters, he and Maria looked like a couple on the way home after a perfect day out: lunch, followed by a stroll in a park, a drink, a film, dinner, a nightcap and now these moments of giggling foolery before bed, and the hot, sour smell of each other in proximity. The feeling was so real for Alex; he knew he had to make it come true. He took Maria's hand and put his face into her hair, kissed her lightly on the neck and refrained from suggesting a midnight marriage, but did say they ought to wangle an evening off together and do all those perfect-day-out things. And she squeezed his hand and licked his lower lip and kissed him, and said, "When? Just tell me when, Alex, and we'll do it."

When he got home, he looked in his mirror, and that ludicrous lovelorn look in his eye was gone; he would be Alex the lover, once again.

TWO

What can I get you? Same again?
There is now a gin menu – yes, a carte.
The gin is à la carte. The food is not. The food is basic, and recently thawed, and often microwaved, and overpriced, if I'm honest. I'm not, though. I work in catering.

The penny dropped mercifully quickly to reveal that Alex's perfect day out with Maria Betancur had never been destined to get beyond the scatter of a few words and a kiss on a late-night train. She was never going to look his way with anything other than friendly detachment, so he resolved to leave the Solano. It was not just because of Maria's proximity and distance rolled into one, he had to admit; with its poncy bottled beers, brash New World wines and gaudy cocktails, it was not what Alex regarded as a proper bar job.
The end of his first winter in Madrid was cold, rainy and dispiriting. Alex longed for some light and fresh air. He briefly revived the idea of heading down to one of the coasts, but did not want to work in a bar frequented by

holidaymaking Brits, nor by the expats he had seen in Mojacar, rabbiting on about their old bank robberies, middle-age maladies or difficulties in getting hold of Branston pickle. The men had been brown and bloated like school basketballs, the women like leather handbags. Alex had seen lighter-skinned Africans than some of the *costa* Brits, and that alone made them absurd and would stand in the way of establishing a respectful relationship with them. After another trudge around the city centre, Alex got a job in a bar called Señores, off the Plaza Mayor in Madrid's La Latina district. It glowed on and off all day and pulled him into its pulse, leaving him without time to dwell on the dark, damp days and the absence of Maria Betancur from his life.

Those days were split by the *siesta*, plus *ad hoc* breaks if Leon, the manager, saw Alex red-eyed and on his last legs. It would take years for Alex's body-clock to get used to a *siesta*, so in spite of being dog-tired, he often failed to sleep, got up, got dressed again and wandered, got a feel for the city that he had not sought out when working either at the Cambridge School or Solano. He found a new curiosity in its buildings great and small, its wide streets and its narrow alleys and its people, young and old.

He sometimes conjured up Maria's voice, the laugh in it that was always waiting to be summoned, but not often. Sometimes, he looked for her among the passers-by, but mostly not; he was mostly over her.

At work, Alex became familiar with the bar and its punters and what they drank and ate, whether they liked to talk or be silent, and when. He waited tables sometimes and helped the chefs prepare *tapas* and full *raciones* if there was a rush on. He counted off stores as they were delivered. He wiped surfaces and mopped floors intermittently till close of play, going round customers to bring their evenings to a gentle end.

Home was rent-free in a small room nearby, in a block owned by señores Hernandez and Delgado, the bar owners. Alex shared a bathroom with a passing cast of migrant workers whose business was probably not mysterious, though never quite clear either. There was the rumour, and occasional smell, of a kitchen, but Alex ate his meals at work. He was more exploited than he had felt at the Cambridge College or the Solano and had far less time to himself. For some reason, he loved it.

"He's a bookbinder by name and not trade, a mathematician only in name too, and that one an affectation, anyway."
"Yes."
"Though of course, only affected types even know the word affectation and that people... adopt affectations. Like a child. Or a cat."
"A kit?"
"Ha ha – no. A cat."

Leaving the Cambridge College had triggered the loss of Alex's circle of friends. He had felt that their attention was never quite in the moment anyway. They made a joke out of everything and yet suffered the flaw of not really having a sense of humour. They drank too much, Alex thought – saw them as a barman, of course – going weekly through the stupidity of the same actions followed by the same regrets. It was easy to effect a culture change and drink Spanish-style; in Spain, drinkers were not expected to get legless, as they were back in Britain, but Alex's colleagues treated this as a challenge rather than an opportunity. Their entreaties to stay in touch had been half-hearted, though not in an unkind way; moving on and forgetting, and being forgotten, was just the way of TEFL teachers abroad.

The only one to keep in touch with Alex was a guy called Matthew Bookbinder. He had left the school soon after Alex and got a job at a new school near Señores. Math was short and thin, a feral look to his face and his stance. He reminded Alex of a child watching an insect, interested in its appearance and actions but also in whether he'd be quick enough to kill it when he got bored. He forgave people who called him *Maff*, but he liked them better if they did not. Students had complained that he was over-formal, rarely deviated from his lesson plans and neither cracked jokes nor sang songs, to which he said, "Look, I'm not there to be their *friends*, mate."

One evening around nine in Señores, Alex heard the shouted order, "A small beer, mate, in four separate glasses."

"Long as you pay with a four-Euro note." Alex approached, hand outstretched. "But this one's on me."

Math was in just after classes had finished. He had a few years' TEFL behind him, so never hung around after class analysing lessons.

"My students, whoever they are, wherever I am in the world, get the same lesson all the time," he had confided to Alex. "Too lazy to progress? Suits me. I'll teach them anyway. So, but never mind *me*. Hey, does this place suit *you*? It's kind of... *dead*?"

"Allows me to skive and talk to you, though." Alex did not mind the downtimes. They made up for the frantic lunchtime and rush-hour trade.

"Do you get the students in, from our school?"

"Sometimes." Alex had noticed a few studenty types in after classes.

"Two whole streets away." Math raised a thumb. "But right below the school they have a miserable, overpriced little bar smells of cooking oil, so they head there because it's *easy*. I told you they were lazy?"

They were interrupted by a customer, who stood next to Math at the counter and ordered a white wine, in English. As she looked assuredly Spanish, Alex's vanity was pricked, but in truth he enjoyed any respite from speaking his still-halting Spanish. He served her wine.

She was tall and thin and slightly stooped. She reminded Alex of Popeye's girlfriend Olive Oyl. Her black hair was wiry, somewhere between short and long, and looked as if she had cut it herself in a bad mood and a hurry. She wore a frumpy, lacy blouse and yet still looked slightly boyish.

Math had a frank way of looking at strangers that verged on insolent: at women like he wanted to fuck them, at men like he wanted to fight them. He claimed to be unaware of it. He asked the woman at the bar if she had a cat.

"A kit?" she said. "What, like a *gymnastics* kit?"

"A pussy," Math said.

"*Pussy.*" She looked at Math properly for the first time and in doing so seemed to be aiming the word back at him. "No. Why?"

"Well," Math said to Alex. "She's not a lesbian, then?"

Alex made angry eyes at Math.

"That may or may not be true," the woman said. "But I know *you* don't have a pussy."

"No." Math held his hands up. He was about to do his *hey-can't-you-take-a-joke* thing that Alex hated. Alex had put up with that kind of thing along the course of his whole life: lame gags about being white, about being black, about being neither, or both. He forgave Math easily when he did it. He sometimes wondered why.

The woman said, "You just *are* one."

"Well." Math paused, then grinned. "Too-*shay*."

"Math." Alex appreciated seeing Math being bested, but not from mixing it with a customer, on Alex's watch. "You're out of order, pal."

"Sorry, mate." Math bade Alex pour the woman another white wine.

She watched it being poured, said, "I won't be drinking all *that*. Got to leave some for you Australians, or you'll have..." She searched for a word. "Tremors."

"Kiwi." Math pointed at himself. "But close enough."

Alex added the wine to Math's bill.

"*Geographically*, anyway."

Into an awkward silence, Math stuck his hand out and introduced himself. The woman looked at it for a second then shook it in a way that got Alex smiling; it was as if she was doing a *wanker* gesture. He sought a professional distance, but she looked at him searchingly then offered him her hand. She did not shake it in that mocking way, just pressed it saying, "Nuria Hidalgo. Not a lesbian." She rolled her eyes towards Math. "So far."

∼

An hidalgo *is a member of empire-building Spanish nobility. The feminine form is* hidalga. *An* hidalgo *is a noble with no hereditary title. Los hidalgos didn't have to pay taxes. They developed a reputation for owning nothing, except the world around them, as long as they occupied it with grace.*

  Sometimes Alex was in the conversation, sometimes not, when he had to perform his tasks. Nuria Hidalgo lived nearby, he and Math found out. She worked in the admin part of El Corte Inglese at something boring and spoke English with a rollicking carelessness.
  True to her word, she had not even finished her original glass of wine by the time she was readying to leave. Alex was busy with a customer at the other end of the bar, so Nuria walked around to wave goodnight and to explain that the friend she was waiting for had arrived. They were going on, she joked,

to a place where they didn't let New Zealanders in.

"Sounds like a plan." Alex spread his hands. "Listen, I'm sorry about... you know..."

"I can handle *him*."

"I saw that – you *can*, too."

She went back through the small crowd that was filling the bar. Alex turned his head just in time to see Nuria towering over her friend as she greeted her. He had to be seeing things, because just before they stepped out into the night, he could have sworn that Nuria's friend was Maria Betancur.

"*It just looks like... lines.*"
"*All art is just lines.*"
"*Like... scribble.*"
"*It's all scribble.*"
"*The Mona Lisa?*"
"*The one in the Louvre?*"
"*No. It's in... Paris?*"
"*Yes?*"
"*I suppose that's scribble, too?*"
"*Sure it is.*"
"*So – what – I can buy it, then?*"
"*The Mona Lisa? For sure. Come back at six. It'll be ready for you.*"

Señores did indeed suit Alex. He got to know the regulars, their orders, their quirks, their repeated stories that were not worth telling. One was the owner of a nearby gallery, who had made the news because a millionaire had walked into his shop and bought everything, in turn creating another millionaire. In fact, he had needed to clear the shop for damp-proofing so thought the tale up as a publicity wheeze. Nearby shops were in on it and some other dealers, prompting rumours of art flooding the market – the words *unknown Picasso* were bandied around. Consequently, Señores attracted journalists, art dealers and the plain curious. The story had attracted envy, and the ruse had been unmasked, though nobody was sure if this revelation was not itself part of the plot.

Alex often had to tread the way of the philistine and admit that he did not *understand* art; he tried not to say it aggressively, nor to make a virtue out of it, allowing that it was his own fault. Privately, whenever he saw something along the lines of what he called 'shapes and spaces' he was tempted to give them a bit of life with some stick-insect figures. He was saying this to one of the visiting dealers idling at the bar one day, a Belgian. The guy laughed and said, "I know what you mean."

Alex understood by then that the dealers did not necessarily like the art they dealt in.

"It's like your job, in a way," the dealer said. "You have all these drinks here." He pointed at the array of bottles behind Alex. "But I'm sure you don't like them all." Sure enough, there were many Alex had never tried. "In fact, it'd probably be a bad thing if you liked them *too* much, eh? Same with me, eh? I'd have a house full of art but no money. Here, I'll show you something." He heaved a medium-sized portfolio up onto the bar. He looked from side-to-side, wary, Alex supposed, of competitors – though a lot of them were simply habitual show-boaters – and bade Alex lean over. He pulled out a few sleeves of acid-free paper folders and opened each one, revealing the works inside.

"You see them?"

Alex appraised and dismissed them quickly. He said, "They look like... squiggles."

"Squiggles?" The man considered the word and looked pleased to have either learned or remembered it. "Yes. Anybody could do them, right?"

"For sure."

"Wrong. Here." The man pulled out a pen and handed it to Alex. He extracted a paper serviette from a dispenser on the bar. "You draw one."

"Okay." Alex was glad to accept the challenge. The dealer held the folder open, and Alex copied the squiggle as closely as possible. He took his time; he knew what was coming, of course, but he enjoyed taking part. He finished it and showed it to the dealer.

"Happy with that?" the man asked.

"Sure."

"So how are they different?"

"Tell me." Alex laughed.

"I sell this to the right person." The dealer tapped the folder gently. "I get thirty thousand Euros. It's by Dali. You've heard of Dali, of course."

"Well, sure." Alex had never been keen on what he had seen of Salvador Dali's work – floppy clocks, ants everywhere, people with drawers in their torsos, what was all that about? – but everybody had heard of him. Even undiscovered native peoples in the Amazon Rainforest probably had a Dali print nailed to a tree. The dealer told Alex that, towards the end of his days, Dali began lots of drawings, but his old-age attention had often wandered mid-stroke, and they had been abandoned, though not before a sketchy alliance between dealers and Dali insiders made sure that he signed them. Squiggles, then – a good word, found by Alex – but they were still by Dali, leaked onto markets through his estate or, sometimes, via past students of the master's, their souvenirs turning into money-spinners.

"So, Alex." The dealer had rolled Alex's work into a ball – a perfect little work of art in itself – and tossed it. "*Yours* is a – what did you call it – a *squiggle*. Mine's a fucking Dali."

He lost an arm in a faraway war, while successfully dodging a bullet – walked into the outer circle of a Valmara bouncing mine.

"Victim-operated," he complained to anybody who would listen. "Except in this case it was some other... fool *who set the thing off." He sometimes forgot the war, just sensed the question:* what were you doing in Mostar, anyway? *It lurked in the recesses of his mind, glowed each time his shoulder ached,*

each time he went to scratch the missing limb. The Croatian military were fellow Catholics. Wasn't that enough?

"But you never set foot in a church," people said, when they got drunk and let fly their resentment of him. He missed his arm. He wondered if it had ever gained its own agency, if it would have missed him. But only when he, in turn, got drunk. Could it have? Not so much, he had to admit – not so much. Even he hated himself, what was left of him, when he was drunk.

There was entertainment value from the other customers, many of whom liked to talk if they got the chance, if there was a silence that bore down on them and oppressed them, perhaps, or some spark that ignited a need to roll out their stories. Just like on the *costas*, one punter was rumoured to have been a bank robber, home-grown, who took part in a celebrated robbery in Nice in the seventies and had lain low ever since. Another had been a high-profile communist who had been caught living the high life and had to renounce his earlier zeal, though he still claimed to have it whenever he was drunk. In contrast, there was a woman who had interpreted between General

Franco and any world leaders who had been arsed to know his words in English; still nobody wanted to know what he had said, and she seemed aggrieved about this at times. She was kind, though, Alex thought, often walked a dog for an infirm neighbour, one of those wrinkly dogs that looked as if it needed ironing, who sat patiently by her stool blinking out at the world, always looking slightly unhappy, it seemed to Alex, as if aware of its own ugliness.

Another regular was a middle-aged amputee called Ramirez. Alex knew he was an amputee, because that was how he introduced himself. To Alex, it was like introducing yourself as *the black guy*, or *the fat lady*.

Math asked Ramirez, "So what's missing, mate?"

Ramirez explained patiently, "My left leg."

And before he could set off on his usual explanation – an industrial accident, the horror of which, Alex felt, he made himself relive each time he told the tale – Math said, "Spanish Civil War?"

Ramirez said, "What? Do you know when that war occurred?"

Math said, "Mid-nineteen thirties?"

"Well, yes." Ramirez looked slightly disappointed not to be able to correct Math. "To be in it, I would be ninety now. How old do you think I am?"

Math guessed, "Eighty-nine?" and apologised tacitly by buying him a drink but christened him 'What's-Left-Of-Ramirez'.

Ramirez insisted on trying his English out on Alex, who mostly did not mind. He often got it wrong, though, and always wanted to be corrected, he claimed, yet hated it when Alex did so.

"Thank you," he said to Alex, of a sandwich, or something. "It was formidable." Alex was not in the mood for explaining that the English word was not the same as the French one. At least Math was on hand to check with Ramirez, "What, you found it *intimidating*?"

The señores' wives sometimes made state visits, women who said little and laughed mirthlessly. They sported big hair and had a tendency to be overdressed – looked like a million dollars, as Math whispered, Australian. They had thin faces with small features and yet had double-chins, showed yellowing teeth marked with lipstick, were walking paradoxes with scrawny hips but fat legs; there was no way they could carry themselves gracefully, in theory, yet they defied their own bodies and did. The silence in which the señores sat with them could have marked either contentment or tension, and they reminded Alex of the stern wives in the Laurel and Hardy comedies his parents had for some odd reason found so funny. He noticed with some amusement that, when the señoras dropped in, their men just *had* to catch up on a lot of those little jobs that otherwise might have piled up.

They all filtered in and out of Alex's new world, their stories a jigsaw whose details came into focus then blurred again. Alex did not care who they were or what they had done. He served them and that was it, and it was why he was there. Most of them kept a distance that Alex approved of. In the Solano, a lot of them had wanted to know his name, not just as a precursor to a chat-up, but because they were younger, less formal and more open-minded. He preferred the distance. One of his earliest memories of cringing was a family visit to an American-style restaurant in Covent Garden, with the server bouncing over to greet his dad with the words, "Hi, I'm Jamie. What's your name?"

Jeffrey Dante had said, "You'll know my name when I pay the bill, young man. It's on my credit card."

As well as the trade drawn by the art renaissance, office workers came in for lunch and on the way home. Sports fans came in to watch matches on the few small screens, mainly soccer but also, mystifyingly to Alex, softball. He watched the exuberant Spanish fans jigging about on TV, faces painted red and yellow, and thought, *who the fuck would care about* softball *that much?*

"*Where's me fookin' sandwich?*"
"*Kitchen, please purvey Her Majesty her fucking sandwich, please – by royal appointment.*"
"*Eh?*"
"*Meaning, quick, like.*"
"*Oh... aye. Coming up.*"

As it did at home, football sparked an interest in obscure geography. Spaniards knew as much about Newcastle as Alex knew about any city in Spain other than Madrid, but football fans asked, not facetiously, as far as he could tell, if Alex had met Paul Gascoigne during his time in the city. He was able to tell them in truth that he had: Gazza and his publicist had come into the Hedgehog one day, a quick pint-and-a-bite stop before some charity thing he was doing nearby.

Gazza asked Alex, "Where's me fucking sandwich?" It was not a nasty swear; the footballing legend was wearing his playful *fuck-off-Norway* face.

When Alex shouted, "Where's Mr Gascoigne's fooking sandwich?" through the kitchen hatch, the legend made his gummy laugh and leaned over to shake Alex's hand. Alex told the same story if anybody asked him about any British celebrity. So far, he had told it about the Queen, Princess Diana, who had died when Alex was eight, James Bond – any of them, he supposed – and Kylie Minogue... who was not British anyway. Not one person had questioned it, not even for the Queen.

Math came in with his students sometimes, usually wangled a drink out of one of them and left them to it. He sat at the bar, bent Alex's ear and got into conversation with anybody who hovered nearby. Alex kept an eye on him to make sure he was not winding them up.

"What's that?" Math pointed to the *tapa* one of his students had ordered.

The student looked to Alex for help. Alex enjoyed sending up the menu's crap English translations, so common they had to be a Spanish tradition, so duly rendered the dish as "Aubergines, striped by hellfire, traumatised by olive oil, scatter-gunned with cayenne pepper. Just in case that sounds negative, I recommend it, Math."

"Aubergines?" Math did not laugh, just shook his head sadly. "Alex, they call them native *Australians* these days?"

Alex was happy enough to walk into Math's gags. They were throwaway enough to forget at once, so he was soon able to laugh at them all over again. They were also preferable to Math being morose. Alex sensed melancholy in his friend, that he was pissed off with the job, and probably with Madrid, that he was fixing to leave. If Alex was especially busy, Math did not walk the length of the bar to say goodbye, just left. Alex would check that he had paid his bill – you never knew, with Math – and forgot him till next time.

As his downtime commenced and he ate his evening meal on the punters' side of the bar, Alex watched the television evening news. He sometimes found himself casting a hopeful eye on the door for the elongated form of Nuria Hidalgo and her little shadow and – because he had forgotten Maria Betancur, had he not? – wondered why that should be.

"To be honest – I'm not going to lie to you – to be honest –"
"Don't be honest. I want what everybody wants. I want lies, and flattery, and the illusion that everything is good and, for however long it lasts, the best gloss you can put on things."

Back at the Cambridge College – a foggy age before, it seemed to Alex – he and Math had gone within a few days from nodding terms to Math asking Alex,
"So, are you merely angry that this shit job is not what you thought it'd be, or on the way to suicidal? Bitter? Or just plain puzzled?"
Math was from Auckland. He hated the way *Matt* got elided to *Maff*, poised between the *t* and the *th*. He liked Math because it was easy for Spanish people to say, with their habitual *th*.

"Or because you're pretentious?" Alex suggested, which pleased Math because, being what he called plain-spoken and what most people called rude, he appreciated directness from others.

"Have you done any of the girls, uh... *in-house* yet?" he asked Alex during their first escape from their colleagues in a bar a few streets from the Cambridge College. He meant the school's more-than-fair share of earnest Home Counties types of women who drifted into TEFL, and went off on one about how the Brits at the school hung out together and shagged one another in circles reminiscent of incest because they were afraid to engage with Spaniards other than by means of the imparting of English. Alex felt that Math was a bit harsh on them, but not strongly enough to argue their case. His rant was also funny – nearly always forgivable.

Math had no plan, he confessed, he just knew that he was not going to spunk away his twenties in Auckland. He was bi-polar, Alex realised. Perhaps his being able to make Alex think and laugh in almost equal measures was a product of his condition. Alex would have been friends with Math, he thought, wherever they had met; Math was not one of those McFriends one got stuck with due to the happenstance of work abroad.

Of all Math's qualities, Alex liked his honesty. Jeffrey Dante had told Alex once, "If you have your honesty, then you can never lose everything. But it's a double-edged sword." It was the first time Alex had heard the phrase. "If you do good things," Jeffrey had continued, "then you can always be honest about them." Those words came back to Alex often, but especially if he was witnessing the double-edged sword of Math's brand of honesty.

Everybody wants to be counted among their friends, except when they are guilty. Everybody wants friends, until they let you down, and become guilty of acts you may not approve of. Everybody wants their friends to be a mirror of themselves: guilt-free. Because everybody is guilty, and everybody is guilt-free at the same time.

Behind the bar, there was little that took the smile from Alex's face, even if it was sometimes fake. In the Hedgehog back in Newcastle, he had got an unfair share of stick, he thought, for being a Londoner, for being young, being a student, for working at the planning department – a *shitload* of invective for that – for being black, and also, of course, for being of mixed race: his natural politeness mistaken for weakness. He had stood up for himself with the support of the manager, other staff and quite a few of the punters. In Madrid he had liked Solano because, once the doors opened, there was no time to do anything other than serve drinks; it went literally without saying that there was no time to be hassled.

Back in the Hedgehog, there had been men who had come in not just to drink, but to vent at people – anybody. One guy pulled Alex over the bar by the collar once, ripping the shoulder-seams of his shirt, because, he claimed, Alex had left a millimetre of his pint unpoured. Another wore braces and deliberately sat near the door, knowing that at least one pissed punter would have a cracked light-bulb fizz dimly to life in his brain to illuminate the idea that it would be enormous fun to give the braces a twang, therefore drawing, and probably deserving, a punch on the snout. The fights always occurred outside and usually broke up quickly, but all the same, there had been a constant undercurrent of violence to come. There was categorically none of that in a place like Señores, whose customers could be loud and opinionated, but were rarely drunk on their one or two glasses of wine, sherry or beer; it was the usual Spanish way.

Coming back one day from a walk, Alex was perturbed to see that What's-Left-Of-Ramirez was still in the bar and looked as if he had imbibed more than his habitual pair of lunchtime sherries. When Alex greeted him, he peered at Alex in a drunkard's who-the-actual-fuck-are-*you* way. Alex looked up and down the bar and saw that nobody else was around. It fell to him to suggest that Ramirez go home and sleep it off.

Ten minutes later, with the aid of Leon, señor Delgado and Lucky, the largest chef they had, Ramirez had been talked into silence. He had left several smashed glasses and two overturned chairs behind him. He had offered Alex the usual insults on his way to being poured into Lucky's car. He had also mentioned Alex's horrible friends, coming in and throwing their weight around, which had drawn a glance from señor Delgado; however, it had ended with the señor rolling his eyes.

Alex had just one horrible friend – well, had just one friend, really: Math, of course. He was surprised that anybody could take Math *that* seriously, to ruminate on anything he had said and get fighting drunk about it. Math could be merciless in his approach to the locals speaking English, but it was not personal. It was like joining a running club for Math, Alex thought; if you kept up, that was good, but if not then you were fair game for a bit of gentle scorn. Of course, some people took scorn very seriously, no matter how gently it arrived.

"I drink to remember, not to forget."
"To remember... what?"
"I don't know. I haven't drunk enough yet."

Most of the drunks in Señores were harmless, and having to chuck one out was shocking. Alex did not understand the unhappy drunks. He felt that he *should* have: those who swallowed a skinful then called up memories that made them cry, and the fixated ones, who thought up all kinds of plans, to travel to Peru, decorate the flat, buy stuff on eBay that they already had, repair the car – right this second – and the nostalgic ones, who texted exes, estranged friends, parents, and children at three in the morning. They were all charmless, and yet the idea of chucking them out was almost inconceivable.

A glass of red wine helped. Alex would get over it, but the last thing he needed was the entry of a punter from Solano. Alex had forgotten his name. He had bent Alex's ear once in a rare moment of downtime, by listing the bad qualities of some guy who had spurned him, or whom he had spurned, or... fucking *whatever* – Alex had not been particularly interested, but he remembered that *negro hair* had been among the absent guy's qualities – bad or good, Alex could not recall. When Alex had laughed at this *faux pas*, somewhat disbelievingly, the guy had assured him that he didn't mind such hair on real negroes. "Seriously?" Alex had teased. "What, real *actual* ones?" If that was a chat-up line, it had been a disaster.

Luckily it was plain that he did not recognise Alex. Alex was relieved that he had not been stalked. The guy looked through him, passed on, sat at a table and called a waiter. Alex kept half an eye on him as the evening rush built up. A young black guy joined him. Alex was amused to see that he had straightened his hair.

Alex had seen Math wind up various people – not only Ramirez and Nuria Hidalgo, but also some of the art gallery customers and, he had heard, one of the señores. Math may have been his only friend, but he could not come in upsetting people. He was going to have to bar him.

The finality of the decision oppressed him but also lifted him. It was good to know what you were going to do. And so, what *about* Nuria Hidalgo, now that the thought had come to mind? Alex had been keeping as keen an eye out for her as a busy job allowed. He was fairly sure that she had not been in, if less sure why he was even bothered. So she may have been a friend of Maria's – so what?

But perhaps he had given in too easily? It was bullshit, okay, and he did not like to stereotype people any more than he liked being stereotyped, but was it not said that Latin women liked all that noble tilting-at-windmills shit, liked to be wooed and won? Perhaps Alex should have been more proactive in seeking a liaison with Maria. Well then, he would be, if he got the chance again. He was troubled by the challenge but satisfied that his thoughts had ended in a direction he could follow.

"Hey, hero." A customer was standing at the bar, not quite snapping her fingers. Alex walked down the bar to serve her, to greet her, to lean over and kiss her on both cheeks.

He said, "I was just thinking about you."

"I'm sure you tell all the ladies that," Maria Betancur replied.

"No. Really. Wow."

"What?"

"I missed your eyes."

"Thank you, Alex." She narrowed those eyes. She laughed. "You're nuts."

"We should go for that perfect day out."

"That... *what?*"

Alex was thinking of that distant night on the Metro, when he and Maria had fooled with the abandoned office chair, and the background of people thinking he and Maria were lovers... *probably* thinking they were lovers – well, possibly... and his letting them down. Now he had the chance to make it up to them.

"Well, okay. I should have a drink first, though, Alex, eh?"

It's a horrible language. It never stays still long enough to capture it. In that, however, it is just like me. I am my own imaginary friend.

Maria was studying English at the school down the road.

"Horrible language," she reminded Alex. She had rowed with Juan Pereiro at Solano. She had wangled a bar job at the Marriot, so needed a crash-course to brush up on the fluent English she had claimed to have. "I hate it," she said.

"You said I made it sound beautiful," Alex remembered.

"Did I?"

They had been at the bar in Solano, just before opening time, their current positions reversed, she behind it and he in front with a coffee, playing at being a customer for five minutes. She had said it, looked away, looked around, looked down, just as she was doing now.

She said, "I was lying, Alex, I imagine. Sorry."

Alex guessed, "You're meeting somebody?"

"Yes." Maria reached a finger up to her eyelash and, very gently, extracted a tiny line of eye-mucus from it. It formed a string of resistance for a second, then gleamed on her finger, like a snail trail, until she rubbed it onto her thumb and made it disappear. Alex could not work out if it was genuinely absent-minded of her or deliberately intimate, or a gesture of contempt. He decided to interpret it optimistically.

He said, "A friend?"

She said, "I don't usually plan to meet strangers," and hunched her shoulders, made her face mime laughter. Alex pitched in with a real laugh.

He took a look up and down the bar: slow night, half empty. He got the mad idea that he and Maria, and Nuria Hidalgo, of course, could head out for the night. He could leave early, he was sure – Leon owed him a bit of time and would surely do him the favour. They could hit the town, find somewhere classy. Alex had to confess to himself that, now Maria had wandered in of her own accord, he did not really need Nuria there. He was certain that she would be a sport about leaving after a drink or two. He decided not to mention that he had spotted Maria with Nuria that time five, six weeks before.

He said, "Anybody I know?"

"No." Maria laughed, delighted, as if he had cracked a joke. "You don't know any of my friends."

He did, though. He felt clever knowing something she did not know. He decided to enjoy it for a while.

He made the claim, "They'd love me."

"I'm sure they would."

"Want to come out tonight?" Alex was shaking as he got the words out. He hid his hands.

Maria spread hers to indicate her surroundings, said, "I *am* out tonight."

"True." He was being pushy – cheesy, even. He reminded himself about being a wooer and a winner, but it really was not in his nature to get in a girl's face that way. The fight went out of him. A waiter beckoned to him for a table order. As he left, Maria whipped her phone out and thumbed and studied it, the screen lighting up her eyes. Alex sorted his order, served a few customers, did a round of clearing tables.

Leon looked down the bar at Maria when Alex asked him if he could scoot at ten. He whistled softly and made big eyes.

"You go," he said. "Unless they discover this unknown Picasso and we get the world press in, we should manage."

"We could go up town a bit," Alex said to Maria, without a preamble. "You, me and your friend."

"You... wouldn't like that, Alex." Maria put her phone away.

"Is it an *imaginary* friend?" he wondered. "I had one of them when I was nine."

"Oh, poor Alex." Maria laughed. "And now?" She pointed at him the way she had always done when they worked together, as if to say, *gosh, you're noteworthy and witty, a proper star*. "You have an imaginary *girl*friend, maybe?"

She said the word exactly as he had; he remembered her rather disturbing gift for mimicry. He liked it. He laughed and begged her to say it again, just like they said it in North London.

They were interrupted by the arrival of Nuria, who bent and greeted Maria with kisses, then greeted Alex with a handshake and the exclamation, "I wondered if you would be here."

"I'm always here," he said.

The three of them spoke over one another for a minute or two, as both Alex and Nuria explained their previous meeting to Maria, and during which Alex got Nuria her choice of soda water on the house – "Not much house in a soda water," he complained – and topped up Maria's orange juice.

"Not imaginary, then," Maria pointed out, and then the remark had to be explained to Nuria.

"Talking of friends," Nuria said. "Is your friend from Down Under here tonight?"

"Down... *under?*" Maria wondered.

"Down under a rock," Nuria said.

"No." Alex remembered that he had been going to bar Math. He imagined the scene briefly, telling Math not to darken the señores' goodly offices ever again. He could tell him to behave his fucking self, anyway. "Why?"

"I have a mouthful of swears for him, that's all."

Alex laughed. "I can pass them on." At the back of his mind he thought, *eh, what, she* liked *Math?*

"Hey." Maria was looking from Alex to Nuria. "Have I become invisible?"

"Just imaginary," Alex said. "We're in Spain," he reminded Nuria. "We *can* speak Spanish."

"*Some* of us can," Nuria agreed. She asked Maria about the new job, about her classes, and the school. Alex thought he saw Maria put her head on one side; it was a gesture that Nuria seemed to understand. Both of them let out cackles. Nuria said, "Oh *oh!*" The phrase followed Alex around the bar as he went about his business there.

A queen walks into a bar. A royal ouch. It was an iron bar. The unfunny joke that disappointed the would-be teller even before he told it – he knew it would disappoint the never-to-be-a-listener.

"The real queen walked out of the bar," he may have said, later, and that made all the jokes redundant.

Alex felt a little left out. He distracted himself with a glance at the clock, which hit a quarter to ten. He served customers, cleared tables. He had decided to ask Maria again about going out somewhere, and Nuria too – in fact, Nuria was a laugh, would work out the score and leave them to it in her own time. He assumed that Maria had gone to the loo, leaving Nuria alone at the bar, and he went over to her. He brought a tray of empty glasses with him – he did not want Leon to think he had cheekily knocked off before their agreed time – but stayed on the customer side. He started to sketch his big-night-out idea for Nuria, and she listened, amused, then thoughtful. She brought Alex's babble to a halt by saying, "Alex, she's gone."

"What?" Alex put the glasses down.

Nuria said, "She was meeting a friend."

"*Yeah*, but..." Alex tried to lose the aggrieved tone, though in truth he felt like shaking Nuria by the shoulders. "I thought that friend was *you*."

Very reluctantly, he joined her in a laugh. She stared, banged her forehead theatrically. She adopted an almost defensive position, reminiscent of a gunslinger in a western. She pointed and said, "You're *him*."

"What?" Alex's smile was almost painful, but he kept it up. "Who?"

"The guy from the bar – the gay place. Wow, Alex. Small world."

"Isn't it just." Later, he remembered each word said through his gritted teeth.

The clock struck ten. Leon made a wave at Alex from the other end of the bar. Alex took off his apron and threw it onto the dumbwaiter.

"What's up?" Nuria said.

"Eh?" Alex did a comic double-take, as if he had forgotten her. "Oh." He twisted his lips over to one side of his face. It was a gesture he had learned at school, to stop himself blurting out everything that plagued his mind. "Nothing. Listen, Nuria, I'm going out for a drink." He laughed along with her at the absurdity of it. "Come along," he said. "And I can promise you a story that will make you laugh. Not very much, probably."

"What's it about?"

"The time I sold the Queen a sandwich."

"I think I know that one. A queen walks into a bar, and the barman – the barman is you, Alex?" Nuria took his arm and led him towards the door and out into the quarter. "What a story. I can't wait to hear its end. And I don't have to."

Boyfriend: traditional, bigshot, professional, impatient, quick-moving, satisfied... sometimes, vain, rule-breaker, steady-handed. Girlfriend puncher. Alpha.
    Lover: child.
    Englishman: a man beyond the help of Christ.

On the way into town, they discussed the weather, the tourists, the part of England that Alex was fleeing from – "Or is it all of England?" – and the Little Britainers in Madrid from whom he had also put some distance. He told Nuria about how his erstwhile flatmates always talked about going to the 'service area' to get drunk; it was their rendition of the Spanish *cerveceria*, or beer bar. He was never sure if they kept it up as a joke, or whether they just thought it was supposed to be said that way; newcomers took it up, sometimes unknowingly, he guessed. Nuria laughed – none of it surprised her – but Alex got the impression she was also laughing at his subliminal display of his superior knowledge. It occurred to him to think about a drink himself, and he said, "Where are we going?"

"I know a place." She had become the host. Alex did not mind.

"Where did Maria go?"

Nuria refused to be drawn, said they could talk about it later.

She took Alex to a poky little bar he had passed occasionally on his wanderings. It was full of what would have passed for a trendy late-night crowd back in London, though, as it was Madrid, the punters were just embarking on their evening out. Alex was diffident about ordering. He assumed, from their first meeting, that Nuria did not drink much, and was prepared to go easy himself, having lost his urge to chase his unhappiness away with alcohol. She ordered, and informed Alex that they would have a carafe of the house white. He liked it enough to knock a glass straight down.

"I met Maria tonight to get some money from her," Nuria said. "I had to lend her three hundred Euros when she walked out of that place. What was it called?"

"Solano?"

"Yes. She was... stupid to leave when her rent was due, and she had other bills – a fucking tax bill from the previous year, or something."

"Well, she had a row with the manager there." Alex tried to remember what Maria had told him.

"No," Nuria said. "Her boyfriend got her to leave, said he'd take care of her."

"Boyfriend?"

"And then they had a row, and he dumped her."

"Boyfriend?"

His name was Javier Bonnano, one of those Spanish guys Nuria deemed to be *traditional*. He was an executive at an energy company, a professional bigshot. Alex fell into silence as Nuria described him, because he had the sense that she was going to answer all of his questions if he just let her talk. Nuria said Javier wore a permanent look of temper barely under control, that of a man who seemed aggrieved that the world dared to move as slowly as it did when he needed its citizens to get a move on and do as many things as he needed to become... not happy, exactly – he was one of those men who was never happy, exactly, she said, only – sometimes – satisfied. He was too vain for humour, in Nuria's opinion, a man who only laughed at his own observations, and too uptight to trust people enough to be friendly to them. He was one of those people whose basic belief was that the rules were for everybody else. And yet...

"What?"

"She... loves him."

"Christ."

"Christ won't help an Englishman, Alex." Nuria waved a finger. "Christ was Spanish."

"She *loves* him, though?" Alex shook his head.

"If she doesn't," Nuria said carefully, "she gives a very good impression of it."

Javier had apparently punched Maria once, outside some party.

"Christ knows she's... *irritating*, Alex." But Maria had confessed that she had lied about the incident or exaggerated it. Nuria no longer knew the truth of the story; she had heard it told six or seven different ways. "I know one thing," Nuria continued. "Any man that punched me would be in the courtroom, and not resuming..." She paused, and said, "*relations*," with the hint of a giggle, despite her outrage. Alex had almost giggled too; the word had taken on a comic, Spanglish quality. "But Alex." Nuria looked keenly at him.

"What?"

"What I don't understand is why do *you* like her so much?"

Alex's thoughts went something like, *because she's wonderful, and witty, wise, and kind, good-looking... and smells great... great body... nicely formed features and toes and fingers...* All the clichés. He could not say any of them; there was something in Nuria's face, and in his brain, that told him he faced ridicule if he said them. He said, "I don't know." Maria was enchanting, he thought, or more to the point he was enchanted – it was the usual mystery, partly alluring, partly just plain annoying.

"Well... for all the usual reasons." He sort of laughed.

The real question for Alex was what did Maria, lovely Maria, kindness-itself, sometimes, Maria – what did she see in this arrogant fool Alex was hearing about? It had to be an alpha male thing, he decided. Alex believed that a man could only really prove himself alpha if he was stuck on a desert island and had to defend himself from gorillas, or crocodiles, or bears – mad penguins, whatever; being insufferable really would not do it, nor would having the shiniest shoes, the best coffee machine or the fastest car.

"Alex, Maria is... *infuriating.*"

"Well, you can fall in love with people who are infuriating." Alex thought of all the nervy, waspish, black-clad women in the footnotes of his love life. They had described him as infuriating too; the best thing he could take from it being that they had deserved one another.

"*Alex!* You *can't* be in *love* with her." Nuria scoffed. "You haven't fucked her. You can't love somebody until you've fucked them. Children do – teenagers, also, but adults, Alex, can't do that."

"Maybe you're right." Alex picked up the carafe and poured. His hands were shaking a little, he noticed with a slight jolt, but he felt fine. He was glad to be out. He stared across the table at his companion. He was glad to be sharing it with this gawky-looking new friend – and she *was* a friend, without a doubt, with a quality that made Alex imagine, for startling moments, that he had grown up with her.

"Maybe I should forget her."

"Maybe you should." Nuria nodded. "At least for tonight."

She had said the words lightly, but Alex pondered them for a second. The place around them was packed, and music started up, made people twitch, tap feet, sing, even.

He asked Nuria, "What's this place called?"

"Ah," she said. "It's a famous bar here. It's called Il Morto Che Parla."

"El muerto – the *dead*... something... the dead *what*?" It sounded Italian to Alex.

"*Il Morto*. It's Italian," she confirmed. "Madrid's little piece of Milan. The Dead Man Talking."

"Italian? You're kidding." Alex laughed. "Why?"

"I have no idea, Alex. Never mind why. Just don't *be* him."

Showdown at Misery Corner, a western without spaghetti – perhaps with aubergines instead – not good, but not bad, nor ugly, destined never to be made, to leave the question unanswered: how do you solve a problem like Maria?

Alex did not bar Math. In a spaghetti-western-style moment, his first visit after the row with What's-Left-Of-Ramirez had coincided with Ramirez standing at the bar. There was a second of recognition from each man, and then they had greeted each other with a slow nod.

"I meant to ask you," Math slipped in after they had caught up. "Have you seen the pussy girl?"

"Nuria."

"Nuria." Math gave Alex a searching look.

Alex gave him the bare facts about his evening out with Nuria. He did not mention Maria, nor that Javier clown, nor the discomfort that had never been far away, a few hours in which he had been saying goodbye to Maria Betancur, for all intents and purposes. Math assumed he had had a good time, said an exuberant antipodean "Ah *yih!*" in response. Alex looked at him in exasperation, then gave in and laughed.

"Not seeing her again, then?"

"It wasn't... *like* that."

"Like *what*, mate?"

For a short while on that night out at Il Morto Che Parla, Alex had wondered if Nuria's exhortation to forget Maria, even just for the night, had been in her own interests, but the feeling had turned into an ambiguity that had passed in and out of their evening together. A group had come to invade their table anyway, and they had all made raucous conversation together, banishing an evening in a twosome for good. Nuria had an early start at work the next day, she had explained – it was two-thirty in the morning – and even before Alex had time to think about it, she was saying goodbye.

All the same, he had seen Nuria several times. She was the only Spaniard with whom Alex spoke English. She made a few habitual errors but did not care, and he was glad. She grasped idiom well, would say, "I can't be fucked," though she might hit a wall with another variation, and say she couldn't be *asked* rather than *arsed*. She never said such things in the look-at-me-I-talk-just-like-the-Brits way that irritated native speakers. To her, it was just a means of communication and served its purpose for conversational seconds. Sometimes, when Alex came out with an expression she didn't know, she would consider it, either note it or forget it. In a café, he said the meaningless "by all means," to a Brit tourist who had asked could he grab a nearby chair. Nuria had repeated it, said, "But that's... *terrible* exaggeration. All he has to do is pick it up and take it. Why would you *say* that?" Alex had never thought about it. It was certainly borderline terrible.

"We *like* exaggeration," he had confessed.

He was never sure if he enjoyed seeing Nuria only because he could hear about Maria. The more he heard, the less he liked, sometimes – about her petulance, her promiscuity and, most of all, her ties to the awful Javier. Alex often held his hand up and said, "I don't want to hear."

"You *asked*," Nuria would remind him, gleefully sometimes, and told him what he both wanted and did not want to hear, about the money Javier squandered on Maria, the weekends away, the arguments that ended them. "But she's free of him, again."

The news did not cheer Alex much. It may have, a few weeks before. "What is it this time?"

"She was being a bit shy with me," Nuria said. "But I think she fucked somebody at the school."

Alex had always believed that for most people who attended a language school, it was mainly for a chance to cop off with somebody. Maria was beginning to remind Alex of a girl at his secondary school called Olivia Naughton, whose putting it about was legendary. Alex had never wanted to screw her, really, but he had often felt that he was the only kid in his circle who had not been invited into Olivia's bedroom. At least some of his friends had probably been lying anyway, but he had still felt as if he were missing out.

"So Javier is annoyed at her all over again, and will never see her again, and has thrown her out, taken back his door key." Nuria looked up and made a cheerful smile. "The usual things."

With time on her hands, Maria was suddenly in and out of Señores after her classes. Alex looked closely at each of the men in the groups, while trying not to look as if he was looking. Maria draped an arm around this one's neck, did a selfie with another, her head on his chest, leaned into another to hear what he was saying, shared a wink and a smile with another, laughed uproariously at yet another's lame fucking joke... Alex watched; he felt ridiculous. She *would* have to go to the school nearest where he worked, of course. He was a grown-up, and it should not have mattered. It did, though. It was an old story: he hated seeing her and yet was dying to see her. It was like rabies, in dire need of water but being freaked out by it.

One evening, with Nuria looking on, Maria chided Alex gently for his lack of attention. He had dropped the flirting; perhaps he was overdoing the cool exterior. By then he was indeed over her again. Or so he thought.

"He's cruel," she said to Nuria, who kept a straight face. "I thought he loved me."

Alex felt stung.

Nuria snapped, "He *can't* love you."

"Why not?"

"You're not lovable."

Maria looked from Nuria to Alex. She said, "This is misery corner. You're no fun over here." She picked her drink up. "So fuck it." She went back to her language school friends.

Nuria said, "It's true. We're not." She held out a hand for her bill. "I'm not hanging out with people if they don't want to be hanged-out with, Alex. Not her, not you. Let's get together when things *are* fun."

She had a point. Alex was at work, anyway; he was not *supposed* to be having fun. He went about his business. He swept his eyes over Maria's friends. He stalked them with his gaze as they paid and got up and left. He watched the doorway for Javier's baleful presence, and that was how his life went for a while: his face stony, his eyes ahead, never straying towards the door, and yet looking out for them all, for Nuria, Maria, for Javier, for Math.

The green baize, stretching out before one in James Bond's town, and that of the Pink Panther, what is one to contemplate? The black, red and white of the cards, revealed in a turn of elegant fingers, the mesmerising silver ball that rattles out one's fate, even as one watches, unable not to watch. The azure of the Blue Coast and all its mysteries is, up close, a quagmire not of allure, but of aspirations. Exiles like the Rolling Stones and their shifting entourage are exalted, while stateless people from several world wars, a hundred genocides and a thousand refugee crises duck into the shadows and hope not to make a splash in the Bay of Angels. If you settle there, you may get the wrong impression of your luck, and you may be trapped until you can pay your way out. And that will never happen, and it will soon become clear that that will never happen, and yet one wakes each day, impaled on the

wish to escape. From The Outsiders' Guide to Nice and Environs, *unpublished by Lonely Planet.*

Math came in early one evening and made apologetic eyes at Alex, got Alex to ask him what was up. He said he had an offer to train as a croupier at the main casino in Nice.

"I'm away off out of here tomorrow, Alex," he confessed. "Short notice – sorry, mate – but any chance of a night on the town, you and me?"

"This is the closest I can get to the town tonight." Alex tapped the bar.

Leon had left, for reasons Alex was unsure of, and Alex had been promoted. In time, he would be able to work out the rotas so that he could have some time off, but not right then. He was busy asserting himself and learning new things and had in fact been at Señores from early morning till way into the night for a week-and-a-half.

"I'll miss you, Math." He wondered if he meant it. He decided that he did.

"Me too. But listen, Alex."

"What?"

Math hesitated, then said, "Shit – why don't you come too? You'd get a job right away – you could do the casino bar. I'll treat you to a dicky-bow."

Alex told Math about his new status. Math said, "Well, con*grats. But.* A bar's a bar's a *bar*, mate?" He really did not understand. The barman in Alex would have been wasted in a casino; drinks were not what the punters were there for. He also suspected that Math's idea that Alex could just wander into a place like that and get a job was off the mark. Any job in a casino in Nice, no matter how lowly, would be one of those you had to buy, or burrow into for years. And for what – serving rubbish fizz and charging the earth for it, because the punters were not there to drink, were stressed, brooding on their fortunes? And Alex's Spanish was hard-won. He did not want to start again with French. But most of all, whenever Alex thought about work, it was a picture of him learning it, liking it, then becoming indifferent – not even passionate enough to hate it – and finally moving on. He just could not keep doing that. The señores trusted him. He liked them and their bar as much as he had ever liked the set-up in any job and, for now, it was his, and he was staying.

THREE

Alex's father:
Working day and night and in between.
Living and breathing and ticking the boxes and walking and talking and spinning the yarn and recounting the tale.
Speaking in the tongues he chooses, and keeping his stupid mouth shut.
Being a good parent and a good man all round.
Avoiding Great Train Robberies.
And coming out every inch the manager, even in a country phasing out inches.

Under Alex's care, the Señores bar welcomed punters in from the crippling heat of summer, and from the humidity under the chill that signalled autumn. He only spoke English to the international art dealer people, or if a tourist wandered in by happenstance or error. If the mood got him, he indulged What's-Left-Of-Ramirez in his English habit.

"Where is your friend?" Ramirez asked. "The little man?"

Alex had received a postcard from Math only that day. Math claimed to be fine, but *just a bit VFH* – short for Victor Fucking Hugo, meaning *miserable* – among people who brought him their addiction every night and wanted him to *turn it from a curse into a blessing?* The words made Alex laugh but prompted him to remember that his job was similar. But it did not do to be conjuring up burdens like that if you wanted to get on with stuff.

"He went to Nice." Alex found it hard to believe that Ramirez missed Math, then remembered that the man was a masochist. Why else would he keep reliving the accident that had cost him his leg? "He's learning how to be poker-faced," Alex said. "Can't give away what he's thinking at the tables." Alex had often thought that maybe Math was learning the life skill of keeping his stupid mouth shut.

His other English-speaking friend had not been in since the night she declared that there was no fun to be had in that corner of Señores, stuck between Alex and Maria. Well, Alex had no time for fun, anyway – or at least so he told himself sometimes. He had never managed a bar before, true; he had done most of the things required to manage one, but never with the full responsibility. It only woke him up in the night sometimes. His dad had told him that there was nothing to it.

"You know those hospitality managers work day and night and in between, Alex?" Jeffrey Dante had said. "They do it because they don't know how *not* to, man – it's true. They do it because they're paranoid about stuff going missing if they take a day off or about stuff going wrong. They do it because they're arrogant, and they think the whole thing will collapse without them. They do it because they have no family life, or because their family life is a mess. They could sort it out differently, but they don't."

"How, though?" Alex was intrigued. By then he had worked for one manager who fitted the paranoid bill and another who ticked all the boxes – a man whose good humour and happiness was grim underneath, and anxious – whose hovering, nail-bitten presence was disturbing. Alex had often thought, *gosh, does he really not have a life*, without thinking of the obvious answer.

"Paranoid?" Jeffrey Dante counted it off. "Judge your staff well when you hire them, pay them well, and treat them well." Jeffrey's staff had worked with him for years, in an industry peopled by transient workers. "Arrogant? Don't be. Know your place. You're part of it, and you're nothing without the rest of them. Family life?" Jeffrey had caught Alex's eye and laughed. "Love your wife and don't catch the eyes of all those women who'll walk through the door," he said. "Be a good parent."

And Jeffrey was, Alex had realised all over again, down south in Mojacar on their last holiday together. Jeffrey Dante had been a good man all round. A lot of the men at his funeral had been old staff of Jeffrey's, mentioning old boozers Alex knew only from Jeffrey's tales, plus customers whose names had occasionally come up: a haunted-looking guy, pickled from subsisting solely on Special Brew and Barley Wine – and yet lived and breathed and walked and told the tale – another who had played cricket for one of the islands, another who was involved in the Great Train Robbery of the early sixties. All of them with good words, and tears, for Jeffrey Dante.

Alex had never forgotten this conversation. He had relaxed enough to know that Señores was not going to crash to a halt if he came in a bit later or took a day off. He resumed his siesta walks. The extra work even made him agreeable to grabbing an hour or two of sleep sometimes, especially when the heat seemed malevolent and left him with nothing else.

Nuria Hidalgo would be in again, he guessed. It was not like they had argued. Neither had he argued with Maria Betancur. He had been dreading seeing her but then had willed her to come in – with the odious Javier or not – or just with her fellow students. Then he heard that the school round the corner was closing anyway, due to money problems. Perhaps Math had run off with the takings – Alex would not have put it past him.

He had to remind himself that he was not supposed to be thinking of Maria, and yet was plagued by the idle thought that her on-off thing with Javier might finally stay off, and he could be there to be the man of that moment. She knew Alex liked her. She knew where he was. She knew they could have that perfect day out and see what happened.

When he lifted his eyes from the week's accounts and saw Sylvia, one of the part-time staff, serving a drink to Nuria, he skulked behind a pillar for a second. Fearful that she would see him, then fearful that she would not, he put on a smile and extended his hand and emerged, looking, or so he thought, every inch the manager.

※

"How did you get the genie out of the lamp?"
"I said his name."
"That was it? You didn't have to... rub the lamp?"
"Rub the lamp?"
"Or... something?"
"I'm Alex. Not fucking Aladdin."
"It's a fucking metaphor, Alex."

He had never heard of the place to which Nuria wanted to take him.
"Of course you haven't, Alex. It's not a place for you Brits. No fish and chips, no John Bull pub, no English football. I would only show you the secret places, Alex – the best ones. I tossed sticks to tell our fortune," she claimed. "When they fell, they told me that we all needed a break from this fucking town."
"All?"
"Ha – you and me. And Maria."
"What?" Alex had placed the glass he was wiping down very carefully.

"Got your attention, eh?" Nuria let out a snort of a laugh that got her some attention of her own.

"Maria?" Alex felt himself trying to look nonchalant. The look Nuria gave him was kindly dismissive. He felt the blood flood his face. Her sureness cheered him. In between tasks, he cautiously admired his own patience; having not thought about Maria for so long – weeks... well, days, anyway – it seemed right that he should be able – *allowed*, even – to think of her again. Nuria guessed what Alex was about to say.

"He's gone." She put a finger to her lips. "Really, this time. Don't even say his name," she warned. "Maybe he's like the devil in that story, and you say his name too often, and in a certain way..."

"What?" Alex had a vague idea of the story but was fascinated. Here was Nuria, without even a how-are-you, babbling, planning – *machinating*. He was not sure of what to make of her like this. The idea that she was drunk was unthinkable, but there was an unsteady flame in her eyes, and a certain drop to the odd syllable that could have been mistaken for a slur. "What happens?"

"He appears," she said. "So, we won't... provoke him. The sticks fell, told me our fates were all coinciding this weekend, yours and mine, and Maria's."

"Sticks?"

"It's a fucking metaphor, Alex."

So Nuria had a musician friend who had invited her down to a resort in this holiday town on the Costa de la Luz. He was called Indo, and he was doing a gig there; he and Nuria could catch up, and why not bring a friend? There was plenty of room for them to crash. So, of course, she would. She had told him that one of her friends had been dumped by both her boyfriend – no loss anyway, fuck *him* – and her employer Mr Marriot, but again, no matter; she had hated the job, and fuck Mr Marriot too. She needed cheering up. And Nuria had this other friend who, she knew, needed a break, an English guy who worked all hours in a bar...

Alex told her about the change in his status at Señores.

"*Manages?*" Nuria clapped her hands, held them out for Alex to take.

"Sure thing." Alex was disappointed that his managerial gravitas had not worked on Nuria. He tried to look as if managing a bar was a thing he did in his sleep. He took her hands. She leaned over and kissed his cheeks.

"A friend who *manages* a bar, then," she went on. "So even more in need of a break."

"When?"

"No time like the present."

"What, *now*? We can't go down there *now*."

"Don't be so... *exacting*. I mean tomorrow morning. I'll pick you up."

"Well," Alex said.

His first reaction to spontaneity was often an inner panic. He always overcame it, but it had to be faced. It was much too short notice, he was thinking, then reasoned that even if he had *had* enough notice, he might have made some excuse not to go. But Maria was going. All of his contentment at being at a distance from her vanished.

Nuria said, "Well, *what*?"

Alex walked up the bar and begged a minute of the señores, abandoned the story he had been about to tell them then told the truth. He said he would sort out one of the trustworthy staffers to come in to replace him and would be away all day Saturday and back Sunday evening and asked them if it would be okay. And, of course, it was, and with the señores' good wishes.

Nuria said, "Did I just see what I just saw?" and Alex nodded, almost nonchalantly. She grinned widely and bade Alex prepare her bill. She paid and left, reminding Alex to be ready at nine with his inflatable crocodile and his Panama hat. Enervated by the idea, he finished up at Señores that night and was convinced that the coming weekend would change his life.

When he got home and went to look it up, he had forgotten the name of the place they were headed to. He remembered that it was on the Costa de la Luz anyway, which narrowed it down to a mere matter of somewhere between Cádiz and fucking Gibraltar. He did not care; he would be on the way south to the last of the sun, and Nuria would be driving, and he would be in the back. With Maria. By the time they got to wherever-the-fuck-it-was, Nuria would be catching up with her musician friend and he and Maria would – well, of course, he was not going to tempt fate by *presuming*... What could go wrong? Nothing. He would be sleepless the whole night, he feared, but then found himself waking, puzzled at the light that streamed into his room and the slight hint of music it seemed to be tracing.

We knew he was a spy, but we travelled with him. It was the best way to watch him. Later, we could denounce him. Or kill him. Or better still, see if he disappeared into the surroundings in his own way. That way we wouldn't have to think about him, and it would be as if he had never existed. From Bad Advice for People in Times of Stress, *author unknown.*

At ten to nine, Alex was at the corner of his street outside the Señores. He sipped at a *café solo* he had made himself. He nodded at the Saturday morning punters – people who worked in the nearby shops and galleries, and old fellows who had been rising early and coming there since forever – and at the morning staff as they arrived, but he made it clear that he was not casting his manager's eye on them. He enjoyed the feel of the sun on his head. It was strangely exciting to be off on a Saturday – he had taken a whole Saturday off just once since starting there and had not known what to do with himself all day.

He had a day-and-a-half, including a night, to charm Maria. That should have been long enough for anybody.

Alex had never seen Nuria's car. He watched out for a yellow Fiat.

"I'll tell you a thing," Nuria said when she described it, anticipating a question that, to be fair, he probably *had* been about to ask. "Thieves don't steal yellow cars – really. Check with any insurance company." It seemed logical to Alex: a double, treble, quadruple respray job to bury that comical colour. It also seemed to Alex that a yellow car was just a like a big toy and would surely make for a happy journey. It eventually turned the corner at twenty to ten and came to a halt outside the bar. Alex had by then given in to his instinct to manage, checked a few stores, discussed a few chores to be done and errands to be run in his absence. Forty minutes late was not actually regarded as *late* in Spain, so he dismissed the bad-tempered frown twitching at his brow. He put down the inventory he had been studying, waved to whoever might have been watching, picked up his bag and exited, walking towards the car.

Nuria got out of the driver's seat. She said a long, troubled, "Erm," in the British fashion.

Alex said, "What?" but he could see. His face, readying itself to make a smile for Maria, became a ghastly rictus when the fact registered that there was a man in the back seat with her.

Nuria looked down, seemed to be making a decision. She said, "Get in. I'll explain later." Alex caught something in her face that was reminiscent of pain. She looked sorely let down; she also looked sore to be letting Alex down. The look told Alex that she was not in the mood to be cross-examined.

He raised his hands expansively and reassuringly, signalled that they could work it all out. Nuria laughed – or almost, he thought later – and told him not to overdo it. And in truth, he hated himself for his easy acquiescence. He stood there, pondering this. She opened the boot for him. He hesitated, then chucked his bag in, then came around to join Nuria in the front, turning to see a smiling, untroubled Maria and a stocky, curly-haired bloke who raised his hand only very reluctantly for Alex to shake it.

"You know when your metaphorical journey becomes an actual one?"

"No?"

"It's about when your actual journey is reflected in the metaphorical one you've thought of in so many different ways. Do you know what I mean?"

"No."

"No power, no engine, no forward movement, nor the sluggish pace forced upon you by the traffic ever gets near the journey you've rehearsed in your mind so many times. Do you get what I'm saying?"

"No. Just look out the window. And then..."

"Well, that's partly the difference. The... focus is not there."

Nuria had described Javier so well that Alex felt as if he had met him before. Within a few minutes of the journey in the Saturday traffic of Madrid – a crawl, at times, of weekend sightseers dumped off coaches, Saturday school victims and shoppers – it was plain to Alex that Javier's natural way of speaking was that of a man who enjoyed the sound of his own voice. If not the worst Alex could think of, he was certainly in the top five of people not to be stuck in a car with for fucking hours. He had the voice of a *raconteur*, with pauses for the drama of what was about to come, except that he seemed to have nothing to racont that was of interest, to Alex, anyway. Even Maria did not seem *that* interested. Alex suspected that Javier's voice was the same whether he was ordering coffee or addressing a meeting in front of a Powerpoint presentation. He got the urge to ask Maria if Javier ever bellowed sweet nothings at her, or just shouted, "I am now about to present you with my penis."

From Javier's spiel, Maria's indifference and the odd comment thrown in by Nuria, Alex gathered that Javier was going to buy a car down on the coast. His presence was explained, then: the perfect solution for Javier. Alex did not know whether to feel relieved, if that was what it was really about. However, he did not think he was being paranoid in suspecting Javier's motives.

He distracted himself with a fleeting feeling of pleasure, or at least satisfaction, with his understanding of

Spanish. Neither Maria nor Javier was making any concessions to speaking slowly. It even seemed like Javier was exaggerating the odd rolled r, and the odd lengthened vowel; back in Newcastle, some Geordies had done that to Alex occasionally with their usually easy-on-the-ear dialect, so he was used to it, but it was childish and a transparent sign of animosity.

Alex did not want to talk to the fucker anyway... but he was there, and he decided that he would make an effort. He spoke over his shoulder to ask Maria, and Javier, if he wanted to be asked, whether they had ever been down to where they were going. Javier looked at him blankly. Maria said she had, a few times; she had been to Cádiz, anyway. Javier said, "It's late in the summer. You won't get a suntan."

"Don't worry," Alex shot back. "I brought my own." His grandfather Carlton had told him that one; London smart alecks reminding him that the weather would not be as good as it was in Trinidad, trying to disguise their mockery as a joke. Maria and Nuria giggled. Javier scowled. Alex noted it and turned to face the front.

Javier resumed talking to Maria about taking her to some fancy restaurant in Madrid. Alex knew of it – a staffer at Solano had worked there: one of those soulless, pricy places that was patronised, in every sense of the word, by men who liked to show off: a converted monastery with granite walls, for fuck's sake, that only looked good in those shit magazines found on planes, with all the atmosphere of a business-class airport lounge. Mercifully, the conversation petered out in the back. Nuria did not seem to be in the mood for talking but talked anyway, about nothing that Alex could remember later.

"How far?" Alex asked and took in silently that it was six hundred kilometres, while inwardly, bent over, swearing to himself.

The city slipped by. It took what seemed like an eternity to get to the southern suburbs. Alex saw a Metro stop he had never heard of, a train station, a bus garage, and was tempted each time to get Nuria to stop, let him out and let him go back to his life, but the thought was always too late, the prompt fading, so he sat in silence and watched their journey unfold, sometimes as if from outside it.

"*The* fuck *is he.*"
"*Is that an expression of doubt?*"
"*Yes.*"
"*Really? How?*"
"*You wouldn't understand – it's...* Dantesque.*"

A services sign led them to a village somewhere between Toledo and Seville. Alex had lapsed into a torpor induced by the monotony of the road, Nuria's growing silence, the hum of the engine and the intermittent conversation from the back seat. He had ceased to be aware of the route, or even of how long they had been going.

He did not want to eat. He had always found it ludicrous that people on a journey felt as if they had to eat all the time. Nuria probably felt the same. *Look at her*, Alex was thinking, *rake thin, like some ungainly, growing boy*, her large hands and feet, her ugly shirt buttoned up to the neck and yet still with an inch of space between collar and neck, a tug, as she exited the car, to pull her jeans up over the decency threshold. It struck Alex that he had rarely seen Nuria eat.

In the café, Javier pushed on ahead and led Maria off towards the counter, making it clear, Alex thought, that they would be eating their roadstodge at a table for two.

Nuria said, "Twenty minutes, okay – no more."

Javier shot his cuff back and raised his wrist, exposed a watch that was so slim, so golden, it was almost a parody of a watch; its very understatement was... overstated. Javier agreed, "Twenty minutes? Perfect."

Maria turned briefly, waved fingers at both of them, made a slightly comic face, said a slightly comic, "*Ciao.*" Alex was not amused. Nuria let out one of her sharp little laughs, but she was not very amused either.

"*Perfect*," she and Alex said together, missed a boyish high-five but almost managed a smile. She tutted – slightly comically, Alex thought; she reminded him of Basil Fawlty, beleaguered and hapless.

"Before you ask." She held up a hand. "I have no idea."

"Yeah." Alex had plenty to ask. "But –"

"No idea," she said again. "They just came along together. I didn't get a chance to talk to her."

"But he's not gone," he seemed anxious to establish. "Really, this time?" he quoted.

Nuria said, "I told you not to conjure him up."

"*Me*?"

"Well, maybe it was me."

"He's buying a car?" Alex had understood.

"Yes." There it was again, the Fawlty tut: *tch*.

"In... the exact place we're going – *where* are we going?"

"Novo Sancti Petri."

"In Novo Sancti Petri. He's buying a car in a holiday resort, the exact one we're going to?"

"Well, not the *exact* place," Nuria said. "In Chiclana, the nearest big town."

"I mean, he can't buy a car in Madrid?"

Alex saw Maria carrying a tray, Javier clearing a way to an empty table for them.

"The *fuck* is he buying a car."

"Does that mean you don't believe him?" Nuria never pretended to understand something if she did not.

"I bet this car will turn out to be a crock, something conveniently wrong with it, or..."

"Toilet." Nuria headed out of the conversation. "Get me a coffee, for fuck's sake."

Alex got in the queue. He caught Maria's eye across the room. She gave him one of those playful little waves again while Javier made a point, it seemed to Alex, of making a half-turn and looking at him only briefly enough to convey: *are you still here, you clown?*

And Alex *was* a clown. What *was* he doing there? He realised that he dreaded their presence behind him for the rest of the way. He wondered how it would be if he left, cabbed it to Seville, perhaps, and got a bus back to Madrid. Was there even a cab within miles of where they were?

Nuria was out of the loo. She waved to Alex, then made her way through the tables to Maria and Javier and plonked herself down with them without asking, Alex was pleased to observe. He applied himself moodily to his task. He was in a café, but was not hungry; he was a clown, but not funny. He was heading for a musical thing in a holiday resort, but not in the mood for sea, sun or music. When he joined the others and handed Nuria her coffee, she saw the look on his face and broke into a giggle then covered it up like a child. Alex saw that all three of them were looking at him. It was possibly the first time he had attracted Javier's full attention.

"Tell me about this car, then," he said, conversationally. "It must be something very special."

"I'm only interested in things that are very special." Javier fixed Alex with a stare and put his arm around Maria. Alex got it: Javier was the man, and Alex was the court jester, there for his amusement, should he choose to be amused – he *got* it. It was cheesy though, and laughable, and to Alex's gratitude, Nuria hardly bothered to disguise another laugh.

As if he had caught a snatch of Alex's claim that the car-thing was a ruse, Javier began addressing nobody in particular, to explain, "Top-end ex-rental. You know, you go on holiday, you hire a car, but you only go so high in price." Javier let that sink in and, to be fair, gave Alex the chance to refute it. Alex was hardly going to claim that he always went for the most expensive hire car: he had hired cars only twice in his life, mean little chuggers both times.

"Rich pensioners," Javier said. "They use them a few times to trundle to the supermarket, get the stores in for the week. It's a good place to get a car – the best." Javier took a searching look at

Alex. "That's why I'm here," he said. He looked back at Maria. "Mostly."

"Sounds like a plan." Alex tried to look as if he was indifferent to Javier's claim. It masked the fact that it made sense. But why today?

Some of the locals were in, grizzled men with deep, harsh voices, wearing open-necked cotton shirts but thick long trousers from forgotten suits, and heavy shoes and socks, despite the heat. They talked loudly at one another, laughed without much humour, nursed beers gone warm. They sent a glance or two towards the foursome from time to time.

"We're the big event today," Nuria said.

"Today?" Maria laughed. "This *year*."

"Diverts them from the usual things," said Nuria.

"What are they?" Alex asked her, though he had an idea of what she was going to say.

Both Nuria and Maria giggled in a rather unseemly manner. Javier was looking from one to the other of them. He did not seem to be very pleased.

"Country... pursuits." Nuria sensed that Alex knew what she meant. She looked sideways for his approval;

she had managed, with barely a word, to yank Javier's chain.

"Sheep-shagging." Maria made a sheep noise, and rather loudly, Alex thought. He half-expected it to draw at least stares from the group of old men, reduce them to momentary silence, but they cackled on. "Child molestation." She waved a hand. "The usual things."

"What are you talking about?" Javier rounded on Maria.

"Incest," Nuria offered. It was not an answer to Javier's question, just the next thing on the list.

"Religion," Maria said. Nuria burst out laughing, and Javier turned his face to hers. It occurred to Alex that Javier felt his perfect little Maria would not be saying such things were it not for Nuria's influence.

Javier tried to ignore both Nuria and Alex as he gave Maria a short lecture about how rural Spain was the heart of the nation and all that kind of thing, how its old people had endured hardships and ought to be respected and all that kind of thing, and how it was not for hip young urban people to roll into their villages and laugh at them... and all *that* kind of thing. It was strange, Alex thought; it was as if Javier had never heard of such jokes, had never read or watched satire, was unaware of its clichés. Then he realised that it was true: for all his high-flying cleverness, Javier really was unaware of the fact that people got lampooned out of a sense of malice, sure, but sometimes out of affection, too. Maria protested that she was only kidding and Nuria told Javier he ought to lighten up.

Alex kept out of it; the two women ganging up on Javier was enough. The man was his rival – in terms of Maria, anyhow – but they were sharing a journey together, no matter how it had been finessed. Alex felt churlish in denigrating him, to his face, anyway. He had no sure claim on Maria and Maria did not fancy him anyway and... all that kind of thing, and it was a fucking nightmare. He pushed his coffee cup away, drank down his water, pushed his chair back and said in a bored tone, "Shall we get going, or what?" and brought both lecture and protestations to an end.

"*My trip, my car, my friend, my schedule. My unwavering and merciless amusement at the passing black comedy horror of the thing. The cares? The*

regrets? All yours. You are very welcome to them."

Back in the car one of the lights on Nuria's dash kept blinking. She checked Alex's seatbelt then said over her shoulder, "Check your seatbelts, guys." Both Javier and Maria swore theirs were fine. "It's still blinking," Nuria said.

Alex undid his belt, fastened it back, heard Javier and Maria grumbling but doing the same.

"Only takes a dead stop at..." *Seven miles per hour*, Alex thought he remembered. "Eleven kilometres an hour," he calculated. "To throw you through the windscreen."

"Really?" said Nuria. "So... fasten the fucking things properly, then," she called into the back.

"That's ridiculous," Javier said. "Where did you hear that? In England, maybe." He laughed. Maria laughed too. "It's double that, at least."

"What?" Alex said over his shoulder. "Speed is *different* in England, eh?"

"Doesn't matter." Maria was in the mood for a laugh, Alex guessed. "The people who drive dangerously shouldn't be saved. We should abolish seatbelts, and then everybody would drive at a sensible speed."

"Oh, sure," Nuria said. "What could go wrong there?"

"No, really. And the ones who don't, well, we don't care about them."

"Seatbelts save a lot of lives," Alex said.

Maria shot back, "Yes. But lives of drunk people, who drive dangerously."

"The English," Javier said, with some force.

"You don't have to be drunk to drive badly," Alex shot back. "Sometimes it's enough just to be Spanish."

Javier was not stupid; he had been to England, Alex assumed, and must have known that not all Brits drank like they did on their holidays on the coasts of Spain. He probably knew that the UK was a safer place to drive because official surveillance and enforcement on traffic offenders was better than that on murderers, rapists, drug dealers and people traffickers. Javier also had to have noticed that a lot of Spanish drivers seemed to make up the rules as they went along. He was just being arsey and making a point. *Twat.* Alex disliked him even more.

"Touché. Present company included." Nuria laughed. "I hope."

Maria broke out a giggle. The women seemed to enjoy the moment, which left only Javier unhappy. That suited Alex.

The silence went sour as they continued. Alex followed Nuria's satnav gizmo, partly for something to do with his hands and voice, watched for exits and sneaked the odd glance at Maria in the mirror. She sneaked her own looks, laughed with her eyes at Alex but drew Javier's attention, and a tennis-watching movement that went from Alex to Maria. Nuria drove one kilometre under the speed limit. Alex approved, in principle, but was desperate for the journey to end. He longed to see the sign for Chiclana, and at the sight of the first one, let out a triumphal yell.

Nuria brought them to a stop in a car park in Chiclana's dusty town centre. They all piled out. Alex bent and rubbed his knees, reached his arms into the sky, and groaned. He was not too busy with his stretching to listen to Javier. He was still unsure whether to believe the tale about the car but was reassured, reluctantly, listening to Javier on his phone, that there was indeed some kind of deal going down. Javier was getting narked at what he was hearing. He left a voicemail that verged on sarcastic; it did not augur well for a satisfactory business deal, but it was, plainly, about a car sale.

Nuria was adamant that she was not going to wait there for Javier in the event that the seller was not, for whatever reason, going to show up.

"I told Indo we'd be there an hour ago," she said. Of course, Javier was not bothered about being late – even Nuria was not *too* bothered – and he neither remembered nor cared who Indo was, but the exchange at least reminded him that it was Nuria's trip, her car, her friend and her schedule.

Alex was glad to see that Javier had no option but to hang around in Chiclana until he could make contact with the seller. He picked up more harsh words that also pleased him; Maria was going to come on to Novo Sancti Petri. She was not silly. If Javier's deal fell through, she was not going to partake in the faff involved in getting to the coast; she would already be there. She offered some sweet words and a hug, neither of which seemed to pacify Javier.

Alex had almost forgotten the original reason for going to Novo Sancti Petri. Now that his other agenda had greyed out, he remembered that they were going to see Nuria's musician friend do a gig of some kind and hang out with him afterwards. Back in the car, Nuria said that Indo played in a 'sort of world music band' but made his real money by playing what she described as 'Spanish shite' to holidaymakers along the coasts.

"He probably plays English shite, too," she said. "For your fellow Englishmen, Alex. If you make a request, he may even play some shite for you."

Alex laughed. He had a quick rethink about his weekend. Now that it was probably not going to be the weekend he got off with Maria, got her heart or into her knickers or both, he had to take a fresh look at it. He decided that he had better start enjoying it or go home.

Nuria drove them out of Chiclana's centre and over a bridge, then onto a route that looked like a film set representing an exclusive resort town. There were wide roads, elegant holiday housing complexes set back from them and flanked by decorative towers, seaside Gothic and Byzantine, and by evergreen foliage. There were signs pointing to golf courses but no courses visible and certainly, as promised, no English pubs, nor souvenir shops – in fact, no shops at all that Alex could see, nor cafés, nor bars and, into the bargain, hardly any cars, and nobody walking. It looked a little grim and abandoned to Alex. He wondered who on earth would want to stay there – even golfers did not deserve such a place.

"Germans," Nuria said.

Maria said, "Old people, or families. English?"

"No." Nuria said there was no British presence on the Costa de La Luz; the English breakfasts and bingo stopped at Gibraltar, far to the east. She told Alex, "You are the only Englishman for miles."

"You are the last Englishman in Spain." Maria liked the idea. "You are the only outpost of Englishness. Only you can have bacon and eggs and Manchester United." Alex liked it too; they were laughing at last, sharing a joke, and the thing was that it could not have happened unless Javier had exited the car in Chiclana. He liked it even more when Maria leaned over from the back and put her arms around him and gave him a hug and said, "He is *our* Englishman, and we must cherish and protect him."

"Yes," said Nuria. "We'll only sell him off if things get really tough."

Alex got the feeling that all kinds of things could happen, after all; Javier's boss could call him back urgently to his bigshot alpha male job, the Chiclana car seller might take exception to his high-handed manner... and stab him. He could crash the car. On any car journey you were always a second away from potential disaster. Alex looked out at the hedges and fences, the walls and trees, and imagined Javier ploughing into them, a goggled, caped dastard from an old film, his swearing, his getting out of the car to check the damage, unable to stop the steam spouting from the radiator... but willed more sweet words from Maria, and settled back in his seat to enjoy the rest of the ride.

'Men in golfing trousers speaking in golfing accents, talking golfing problems, carrying golfing things. Men eating golfing food and drinking golfing drinks. Men forgetting the wrinkled ungolfing women at home with their bingo punk hairdos awaiting the return of the golfing golfers with their tales of *golfing derring-did.' Excised from the final version of* Fodor's Guide to the Costa de la Luz, *only very reluctantly, because the author – me, that was – wanted to be paid, and the company wanted golfing golfers to go about their Spanish golfing business, safe from the admittedly undeserved ridicule of non-golfing writers and travellers.*

Novo Sancti Petri was gradually revealed by a series of wide roundabouts that led down a gentle slope to the coast. Turnings led to residential roads, and there was no town centre, just a long inland road parallel to the sea, dotted with apartment buildings half-hidden by palms and cedars.

Nuria revealed their destination as the Sol apartment complex. She admitted that she had an address that did not actually mean anything to her. Both her satnav and her phone went into confused meltdown, and there was hardly anybody on the road to ask directions. Each time Nuria tried, she hit on holidaymakers who knew where their own place was but not the whereabouts of any others. It was plain that the map had been printed before the newest holiday builds on the coast. Finally, Alex urged her to drive back up the road to the single bar he had seen. It turned out to be called The St Patrick's Tavern. He was a little surprised to see it; as Nuria had told him, this was a part of Spain into which few British, or presumably Irish, tourists ventured, and it was notorious for being free of all that Costa Brava nonsense. He had to conclude that the locals had welcomed the Irish pub for perverse reasons of their own.

"Get me some Irish stew," he called.

"You're bad," he said over his shoulder to Maria. He had not opted to change seats to sit with her for the last leg of the journey, partly so he could read the map and guide Nuria. He was also genuinely pissed off with Maria for having brought Javier along. His tone was light, but if she had known him better, she would have been able to detect a stiffness to it that revealed his annoyance.

"No," she said. "Why?" But she caught his eyes and invited him to share a guilty laugh with her. "I can't help it." The line was throwaway, and Alex did not feel obliged to respond to it. "You probably only like me because I'm bad," she said.

"No doubt," Alex admitted, and reflected that those women he had loved so intensely had all been bad for him. Perhaps he sought such women out; perhaps he was like What's-Left-Of-Ramirez, and enjoyed reliving the pain each time, just altering some of the conditions. He said as neutrally as possible, "So, what's up later?"

"Later? What, Alex – how do you mean?"

"Are you staying?"

"I don't know." Maria seemed to be thinking about it.

"You *should* know." Alex could not help the hectoring tone. "You know... you shouldn't just wait around to see what Javier wants to do."

"Well, thanks for your advice, Alex. I appreciate it *so* much."

Maria turned and looked pointedly out the window. Alex sat back down in his seat. He had not meant to bring silence to them.

"We'll have a laugh, anyway," he said, but could not even convince himself. Maria acknowledged this only with a sideways glance at him.

"You're right," Maria said. "If it makes you feel better."

"What?"

"I'm bad."

Alex was unsure how to answer this and was saved from doing so by Nuria's return. She looked a little vexed.

"Six different people," she said. "With six different opinions."

Alex said, "Sounds just like Ireland." Or so his mother was fond of saying.

Nuria acknowledged him with a faint smile and said, "Finally, one of them found a brochure." She waved it.

It featured a badly done map with no road names. Alex had to work it out from some of the landmarks shown on it – the local shops and restaurants that had commissioned it. It took them another half an hour of turning all the way around roundabouts and up and down streets of palms and blocks before they found the Sol. Maria seemed to be taking it in her stride and even congratulated Alex on spotting the small supermarket and beach shop that led them to their destination. On the other hand, Alex did not think he had ever seen Nuria in quite such a bad mood as they stopped in the car park and got their bags out of the back.

"We're here, anyway," Alex said cheerily, to neither or both of the women. "Once you're there, you forget about everything else, eh?"

"Of course you do," Maria agreed.

Nuria almost smiled. She said, "Fuck off, Alex. This way, I guess." She raised a finger to both of them to follow her towards the Sol's grand entrance. Alex swung his bag over his shoulder. He was not going to try to both fuck off *and* follow Nuria. He went for what he thought might be the most sensible option.

MA in Tourism: this course offers all aspects of pleb management, and a frustrating job for life in the proximity of any number of the following: the sea, crumbling old monuments, crumbling new monuments, great edifices, shit edifices, posh restaurants, shit restaurants, plebs, transport, bad-tempered service-industry professionals, more plebs – fat ones, thin ones, plebs in unfortunately tight clothes, bald ones, jet-lagged ones, drunk ones, plebs who leave home only to find the exotic, and then complain about it incessantly, plebs with stupid hair, think bingo and disco punk spiky gel dos, plebs with legs that are too pale or too red, shouty plebs, broken-hearted, wall-thumping ones,

exuberant ones, German plebs, British plebs, Spanish plebs, Russian plebs, suitcase-wheeling plebs, plebs clutching small pleb dogs and pleb children and grandchildren, and deep inside, sometimes, pleb foetuses, and... more, all the varieties of plebs there are – ports, airports, bus stations, train stations, and the like. When you complete your course, people will tell you that in their opinion you must find it very rewarding. You will anticipate this, in time, rage against it, and then accept it with stoicism.

The duty manager had been expecting them. He was a large, solid-looking guy called Miquel. He told them that Indo was busy setting up his gear. He said they had beds in the staff accommodation and that Indo would be showing them there once he was ready. Alex got the undercurrent of a bad vibe between the manager and the musician, and he guessed that it was to do with a clash of interests; Alex had worked in places where people's friends turned up to freeload. It could indeed be a pain.

Alex was sure he had seen Nuria pulling on Maria's sleeve, or perhaps it was genuine synchronised peeing, but both women headed for the loo, leaving Alex to hover at the reception desk with

Miquel. Between fielding questions from guests about that evening's dinner and the musical entertainment – all of which could probably have been answered had they looked at the board next to Alex – Miquel told Alex that he had done part of his MA in Tourism in London. Alex did not have a high opinion of people who did an MA in anything to do with the hospitality business: it was simply pleb management. To Alex's mind it was lame to study it. You just got a job and *did* it. He reminded himself that Miquel was only making conversation. He shook himself out of his bad temper and feigned interest till Nuria and Maria came back accompanied by a handsome guy who could only have been Indo.

Alex said, "What – you found him in the ladies' toilet?" He knew that he and Indo would get on when Indo threw his head back and laughed and reached out to shake Alex's hand.

Indo obviously spent a lot of time in the sun. His skin was the colour of walnut furniture, his dark hair bleached to a shade that verged on ginger. His white eyes had the effect of making him look startled, and his white teeth consequently looked Hollywood artificial. He was a skinny little bloke in his thirties, a leather waistcoat over a gleaming white T-shirt, the *bandito* look completed with a wooden pectoral cross. "Just like the original," Alex had once said to a hippy wearing one, thoroughly annoying him. He made sure not to repeat it to Indo.

"I speak English," Indo assured Alex. "No problem."

Alex said, "Cheers," but felt proud when Nuria butted in to say that Alex's Spanish was good. Maria's adding that it was perfect spoiled things a little.

Indo said, "Better make it Spanish, then. My English is nowhere near perfect."

"My Spanish is only perfect in an emergency," Alex improvised. It got a laugh out of them all.

Miquel called Indo over and gave him envelopes with keys in. He kept it all formal, as if they were paying guests. Alex approved – there he was, all hospitality managerial; if people were staying, they were staying, and it did not matter if they were freeloading. As long as they behaved themselves, of course, as expected of any guest.

Indo bade them follow him out into the Sol complex. There were four-storey blocks surrounding groves planted with evergreen shrubs that shone wetly; gardeners had done their rounds, hosing away the dust. The water left the faintest impression of damp on the vegetation, bringing out its perfumes. It was a pleasant effect. Above, people sat quietly on balconies, eating, drinking and talking in low tones behind hung-out towels and swimming stuff.

They turned a corner into the pool area. The pool was a large kidney shape with a deep end. It was one of the biggest pools Alex had ever seen and, after hours in the car, his clothes stuck to him, he wanted nothing more than to jump in.

"Can we use the pool?" he thought he had better check.

An elderly man did a languid overarm stroke. A mother and child paddled gently at the shallow end. There were a few people still on loungers, but they had bags packed and were just putting off leaving.

"Yes and no." Indo sounded uncomfortable. "Look." He had an air of confession about him. "Strictly speaking, people who work here are not allowed to use the pool."

"That's not fair," Maria said. "Are they allowed to admire the plants?"

"It *is* a bit stupid," Alex said.

"A bit?" said Nuria. "It's ridiculous."

"But?" Alex thought he may as well ask, as Indo had left it hanging.

"In practice, some people who work here *are* allowed to use the pool."

"I don't work here," Maria said quickly and happily.

"Like who?" Alex asked.

"Ah." Maria got it. "Like him." She pointed to Indo. "Musicians."

"But not the cleaners," Indo said. "Not the cooks. Not even the men who maintain the pool."

"I get you," Alex said. His heart sank.

"So, *I* don't."

"Indo had an argument with the manager here about it," Nuria remembered.

"Well, good on you," Alex said, but his heart sank even further.

Maria seemed unconvinced.

Indo said, "I'm not going to stop you, though."

"No. Fine by me." Alex was crushed. He had been on the point of hating his weekend anyway; a dip in the biggest and best pool he had ever seen might have alleviated it a little. He hated his weekend even more.

The room was a six-bed dorm, clean and basic, with a tiny balcony. They bagsied various beds and threw their stuff on them, and went off for showers, agreeing to meet at the bar in a half hour. Alex would not swim, then, but for a few minutes he felt wonderful under the shower, though that alone was not going to stop his weekend being shit. He stood there, enjoying the pressure of the water, hearing the barely perceptible music it made. He wondered how long he could possibly stay there, and how long it would take him to be missed, and how long it would take him to shrink into nothingness.

Ein Walter Gropius, es gibt nur ein Walter Gropius
Ein Walter Gropius, es gibt nur ein Walter Gropius
(noch einmals)
Ein Walter Gropius, es gibt nur ein Walter Gropius
Ein Walter Gropius, but his output was copious

In Alex's time in Spain, he had smiled through a lot of Spanish culture because he felt that one should not live in another country and be snotty about the things its people liked. Still, he hoped Indo was not going to be a flamenco act; he did not *get* flamenco – it was just so... hysterical. Who could possibly have *that* much passion?

"Flamenco?" Nuria was scornful at the suggestion. "Of course not."

Maria said, "Thank fuck for that."

Alex refrained from echoing his friends; after all, he was a guest.

No matter what kind of music he did, one thing Alex liked about Indo was his respect for his audience. Its members drifted through the grounds, shuffled in the doors and into the lounge. It looked to Alex like the *Night of the Barely Living Zombie Tourists*, but Indo eyed them appreciatively and nodded to them when they greeted him. It was obvious that he would do his thing at its best whether they were old, young, many, few, dead, or barely alive, clapping and singing along, chucking dead dogs at the stage or just talking among themselves.

Alex observed them sipping at drinks fussily and sparingly, and reconstituting and relighting cigarettes after dropping them into the water-filled ashtrays. They were elderly Spaniards, mainly – Darby and Joan Spaniards – and Germans of all ages over about forty, plus, he heard, the odd Brit, despite what Nuria had told him of the scarcity of them.

There were a *lot* of smokers. Alex was not *too* bothered by them, though every now and again he hoped they would catch collective lung cancer and die and leave the planet to... what? Certainly not clean air. One of those intense girlfriends of his had a father who was fiercely anti-tobacco because his first wife had died of smoking, though he saw nothing wrong with using his car at every opportunity without a tear for all the people killed by stupid drivers. The smokers Alex saw at the Sol under the vines in the garden looked very much like a dying breed, sheep in the shadow of a nuclear power plant, doomed but determined not to mind *that* much.

He rarely saw Germans in Madrid. He observed them at the Sol and concluded, as he always did, that they did not know how to eat or drink: those massive portions of stodge they put away and all that beer, just too much. And the wine they drank was like some mad hatter's parody of wine, like each glass had a spoonful of sugar in it. But they were not afraid of eating it all and drinking it all and had an optimism undampened by anything. They were exactly the kind of people you needed at a holiday resort.

He heard an intriguing conversation – one of those you-just-could-not-make-it-up exchanges – during Indo's soundcheck, a run-through of *You Look Wonderful Tonight.* Alex was glad to have a distraction from such a dreary song. A middle-aged German couple were telling a thirty-something British couple that late the previous night, two people had passed their room singing the words, *One Walter Gropius, there's only one Walter Gropius*, to the tune of the Spanish classic *Guantanamera*. Strangely, they had been singing it in German, but not in such good German that the German couple hadn't recognised it as Brits singing it. It was surreal. Alex soon gathered that the Germans suspected the Brits of the singing – "Actually, where is your room, actually?" the man asked twice, using exactly the same intonation – but the Brits were not confessing and remained enigmatic. Alex had no idea who Walter Gropius was, nor did he find out, as the end of the conversation got lost when Indo climaxed his soundcheck in hiccupping feedback and a drum machine gone rogue, blasting out random drum rolls.

Before Indo started, an ancient man kept moving chairs around near the front, saving them for absent friends and family, guarding them jealously and never getting bored with saying the same thing to impatient incomers who wanted to sit on them. His antics amused Alex, though he could not persuade the women that the spectacle was in any way funny.

"It's not like Indo's famous. Or is he?" he checked, wondering whether Indo had had a minor hit, done Eurovision, sported a mullet, or played one of those annoying-looking guitars from the eighties with no head on it in a video that got played once on MTV and then forgotten. Nuria told him not to be silly.

Indo started off with some Spanish favourites that had sunk into Alex's memory without titles. He was expert at managing to play a guitar and push buttons in front of him for an accompaniment of drums, something that sounded like a bass guitar and a less faithful facsimile of strings and brass. He played songs that were strictly speaking a bit too hip for his audience.

Even so, a hard core of the punters was up out of their seats from the off; some of them looked as if they were helping one another across the road rather than dancing. But they were on holiday and having the best time they could.

Indo started slipping some tunes into his set for the youngsters – "Those of you under fifty," he cracked, and he went into *Sweet Dreams Are Made of This*, *Wonderful Life* and *Big in Japan*, all of which Alex knew vaguely enough to make them sound uncannily to him like the original recordings. Indo also did an obscure Coldplay song – saying the band's name with an MC flourish at the end of it, as if the band had wandered along to this forgotten corner of Spain just to play it – and one by Amy Winehouse about drinking too much that Alex, as a bar manager, disliked on principle.

It reminded him to get some drinks in. He could not make out how Nuria knew Indo – it was just a little too noisy for conversation, but it did not matter. There was a great atmosphere in the bar, and Alex admired the way Indo worked the crowd.

"He's a proper pro," he told Nuria, who nodded. Alex had started to enjoy himself almost without noticing. He looked at the people in front of him, dancing, drinking, having a good time. It did not seem right that he should go all that way and stand among them and be miserable. He resolved not to be, at least until he turned and saw Javier alone in the doorway, unnoticed by anybody, a sour look on his face, making Alex reflect it with his own look, its smile gone.

"New washing machine, huh? Good unboxing? So, what's the – the specs? *How does that baby* wash? *How many revs* per? *What's the rinse cycle* action *– how smooth does that motherfucker* spin? *And what's the, like,* poundage *it can handle? How's the* colour *fastness? You gotta tell me all – tell me* now *before I ex*pire *of curiosity."*

Javier had changed into a pair of jeans in some synthetic material that looked wet. Alex stared at them then caught himself, and nudged Nuria.
The gist of Javier's spiel was that he had got the car, and it was out in the car park. Was Maria going to come out to see it? Maria was not. Alex wondered

how well Javier knew his Maria; he was sure Maria would not care about seeing some car, no matter whose it was. Javier did not seem to be in the mood for a refusal. Alex watched Nuria lean over and put a finger to her lips to bid Javier, "Later." She was pointing at the stage and trying to let the people nearby know that she and Javier were going to shush. Javier gave her an irritated sideways glance and hissed at Maria loudly enough to prompt a few people in the audience to turn and hiss in turn at him.

More and more people were fixing their attention on the little group and away from Indo, so Alex said, "I'd like to see it." He wanted to avoid a scene, sure; he also wanted to prevent Javier from pressuring Maria to go and see the car, because he sensed that once they were out there together Javier would talk Maria into a different evening, out of Alex's reach. He stepped away from the bar, put a foot towards the exit and a let's-go-then look on his face – *I'd-so-like-to-see-your-shit-car.*

And then when he had seen it and admired it, all cosy and pally and best mates together, Alex could tell Javier to drive the fuck off in his nice new car. He could point out to him that if he and

Maria had finished with each other that many times, well then, it was surely the opportunity to take a hint and a hike, find a señorita who did not drive him mad and loved his car and his wet-look jeans and the deepest recesses of his ego.

Alex had never owned a car, and his cheapie hires had been few and far between since he had got his licence. He did not know one car from another. He cared as much about cars as he did about... washing machines, really. If Javier had bought a new washing machine, would he be telling anybody about its exceptional kindness to woollens, how it went from zero-to-forty degrees in three seconds and had an almost silent spin cycle? "Almost *silent*?" Alex imagined saying. "Wow."

In the car park he listened as Javier pointed out this and that. Alex made appreciative noises and managed to find a plausibly banal question or two, Javier's answers disappearing as soon as he gave them.

Alex enjoyed being out in the air, anyway. The evening light was a unique pinkish grey; the lights of their surroundings dotting the darkness beyond the hedges and trees of the complex. Indo's music was a dull background noise, the bass notes standing out.

It was plain that Javier did not want to be showing his car to Alex, but he too did his share of pretence. It was like a distorted mirror: Alex did not care about Javier's car and Javier in turn did not care what Alex thought of it. Alex caught him looking at him at times, telegraphing this very thought. Alex despised it but also found it funny, so he forgave it. He looked back frankly at Javier.

There was a familiarity to Javier that had at first puzzled Alex. He now got the thought that Javier reminded him, a little, of computer reconstructions of some slightly earlier form of man – from a two-thousand-year-old skull or even partial cranial bones found in a bog. He was not ugly as such, but there was something elemental about him that was not going to be redeemed completely by modern life.

Alex had had enough. He pretended to shiver a little. He told Javier he would go back in.

"Well... good car," he managed. "Thanks for... um, showing it to me." Javier treated this to a sneer that, quite honestly, Alex felt it deserved. What he should have said was, "Are you happy now, you boorish... *troll*?"

"You're going back in for that?" Javier raised a thumb. He meant Indo. Almost as if talking to himself, he dismissed Indo as a talentless loser, and why would anybody want to listen to his music? "And fucking *Nuria* – I mean..."

Alex wanted to say, *well*, fucking *Nuria brought you to* – what *was it called?* – Chiclana, *pal.* He said, "What about her?"

"On my case the whole time. Word of advice. You be careful with her."

"Careful?" Alex dismissed the word with a laugh he did not feel like making. He wondered if Javier really thought he was along to get off with Nuria; it was a strange revelation. He forgot it and did indeed say, "Hey, listen. *Fucking* Nuria brought you to Chiclana."

Javier moved shoulders and half-raised a hand, showed that he did not want to discuss anything so inconvenient. Alex treated that to what his mum called his *Picasso face*, shoved his lips to one side to make it plain that he had said all he was going to. He sensed a deep-seated anger in Javier and almost wanted to nudge him the way a friend would, and say, "Hey, come *on* – you're too old for all this... *ire*, man." It was true: once a man was past his mid-twenties, such anger, misdirected and unfocused, looked like the petulance of a ten-year-old.

The two men stood by the car. They were the only people out in the evening, as far as Alex could see, almost arguing, almost wanting not to, while everybody else was inside tapping feet to the music – dancing, even. Alex was definitely in the wrong place.

"Fuck it," he said in English. "I'm going in. See you later."

To Alex's surprise, Javier made a flourish with his key, blinked the lights to lock his car, and trailed Alex inside.

Good car?
Good car.
Good, really?
Good car.
Let me take you away in it. Farewell this time and adieu, you fair Spanish ladies, farewell and adieu, you fair ladies of Spain. And you not-so-fair men, singers of the Night of the Living Tourists – farewell to you too, for by the time your grey heads hit the pillow I will be on the Spanish Main.

The... what?
In my car – it's a good car. Did I mention that?
The Spanish what?

Indo was back to Spanish favourites. The song Alex heard had an anthem-like air of finality about it. Javier said to Alex, "God, I hate this shit." Alex wasn't keen on it either, but he raised a thumb towards the old Spanish couples, some singing, some swaying, a few dancing. He thought it was a great thing, the fleeting community of song brought to them by Indo; it was beyond value.

"They like it," he said.

"But look at them." Javier's smile was devoid of pleasure. "They'd like anything."

Alex thought again what a bleak and unpleasant bloke Javier was. He was mystified all over again by Maria's thing with him, even though he was sure he had promised himself that he would not bother with such a pointless pursuit. Whether Maria stayed or not, Alex hoped Javier was not going to stick around and fuck up the rest of the evening. He stared at him, almost willing Javier to challenge it: it took a lot to provoke Alex into violence, but he really had to resist the urge to punch Javier on the nose.

He could not help but reflect again on how the weekend was not just not panning out, but was managing to not do so spectacularly. He could see no way of rescuing it. Indo's singing irritated him when it came back into aural focus, and there was something about the jolly tune in progress that made him feel murderous. He was angry at Maria for agreeing that Javier should come along; she had just broken up with him, for Christ's sake – what was she thinking of? And Nuria, why had she agreed? He would not have put it past her to agree just for the mischief of it. He and Javier joined the women at the bar as Indo's act came to a close accompanied by loud applause and yells of *bravo*.

Nuria and Maria turned, smiling. Alex smiled back.

"Good car?" Nuria grinned like a boy.

"Good car," Alex said, in the dullest, most expressionless tone he could muster. Nuria exaggerated her enjoyment with a bent-double guffaw.

Javier put on a familiar expression of superiority and plonked himself between Maria and Nuria. Alex had read somewhere that one habit of successful people was the ability to act as if only the people worth their time were in the room; here it was in action.

"Come and see the car," Javier said to Maria.

"The *car*." She made the word into three syllables and seemed to be thinking about it.

Nuria said straight-faced, "I hear it's a good car," and Maria roared laughing in answer. That was surely all she needed to know about the car and yet she extracted herself from the bar stool and picked up her jacket and handbag. She made her little wave at Nuria and Alex and followed Javier out into the night.

Throwing a perfect party or weekend jaunt relies on getting the perfect blend of characters together. Not necessarily people who all get along like the proverbial Balkan country on fire. That would be kind of boring, and we have all been to parties, or, worse, weekend outings during which everybody talked about their mortgages in satisfaction (1980s), smugly (1990s, for a while),

fearfully (early 2000s) and wondering if one would ever take over their lives (late 2000s and on, and on) and been bored out of our minds. A little frisson of friction makes the situation interesting and throws in assertion, and competition, doubt and, sometimes, a drunken episode to escape towards the hope written faintly above the doors to oblivion. The Perfect Hostess Updated for the Modern Gal (but already out of Date), *Introduction to chapter 1, Heather Valdete, Geitzeist Press, 2019.*

Drugs – always *bring drugs.* The Perfect Hostess Updated for the Modern Gal (but already out of Date), *Introduction to chapter 10, Heather Valdete, Geitzeist Press, 2019.*

"Come on, then." Nuria ushered Alex against the tide of grey-haired people in pastel shades and Velcro-fastened shoes. Their music over, they were not hanging around. A few headed for the bar, but most were determinedly off to bed. Nuria led Alex to the stage.

"It was great," Nuria told Indo. Alex echoed her, his voice muted. "I loved it."

Indo grinned. He had probably long before given up, Alex was sure, on the modesty of reminding his friends that he knew it was not their thing.

He acknowledged this by saying, "Got to find some real music, though." As they watched him unplug his little PA system and track down all his leads and roll them up, stick his drum machine, guitar and keyboard in cases, he said there was some live music on at a bar up the road somewhere. It was a jam session, basically, and he had got talking to some guys on each visit to Novo Sancti Petri and promised to go at least twice. And, quite honestly, there was really nothing else to do there in the evening at the end of the season. So why not?

"Sure thing." Nuria looked at Alex, as did Indo.

Alex was not in the mood for more music, more smiles, more exuberant bastards. He would have preferred to go and find Maria, make a last-ditch attempt to do whatever it might take to prise her away from Javier – what did he have to lose? But it seemed obvious that for any number of reasons that was not going to happen. His second choice would have been to follow the Sol punters' leads and flop, head for the room and sleep. It would have been a little ungracious, though... unless he produced a headache. But then what? Lying in a strange bed, brooding; he would get sick of it before it cured him.

"Yep," he said. "I'm in."

He and Nuria helped Indo stow his gear in his room. Alex had assumed that Indo would be sharing the staff dorm, but it was plain that musicians and performers who stayed over were considered a cut above waiting, bar and cleaning staff, and freeloaders too. He had a little room to himself.

"Let's go, eh?" Indo had an air of liberation.

There were a few diehards around when they walked out through the bars and into the grounds, all middle-aged, all German. The old people and families had retired to bed. Away from the bar area, the grounds were more or less deserted. They had an eerie atmosphere, the dark shrubs and trees backlit and up-lit. Indo was not sure which exit to take, so went back in to check at reception.

Alex said, "So you missed Chitty Chitty Bang Bang." In response to the look Nuria sent him, he said, "It was just a car."

"Of course it was. You're pissed off," Nuria stated.

"Well. A bit."

"But... what, Alex?" Nuria adopted the voice of a schoolteacher, probably unconsciously. "I mean, what did you think was going to happen?"

It was a genuine question. Alex, the only one who could possibly have answered it, was not up to the challenge.

"Okay, it's my fault that he came. I'm sorry. It wasn't part of my plans, and I could have really laid the law down and stopped him, I suppose. And I'm sorry – I am. But you need to... *adapt* to how things change, Alex. So you thought, *okay, Maria's free.*" There was an undertone of mockery in Nuria's voice along with her empathy. "After three years with this... guy – this obsessive and possessive guy, you think she just walks away from him and, one week later, two weeks, gets into some big romance with you? Hmm. Is that the story you wanted to tell, Alex?"

"No." If Alex was hearing this about somebody else, the thought came, he may have been laughing. "Yeah. Maybe."

"Prince Charming rescues her from the – the what's it called, ugly giant?"

Alex nodded.

"Under the bridge?"

Alex nodded again.

"The *ogre*." Nuria looked pleased to have found the word. She gave Alex a chance to speak, then said, "I've seen this happen now... five times. Maybe six. A big split, and Maria is free. Javier is cruel, she tells me, tells everybody who will listen. He's a pig, she says. She puts an advert on a billboard. You can see it from space. Three weeks later there they are, lovebirds cooing. Javier will change – he has already changed. Look at the present he has bought her. She puts all that on the billboard. The astronauts will have to change their minds about Javier. Six months later, there she is again. Maria is freeeee, Javier is a pig, again, so there's another fucking billboard you can see from space. But Alex." It was almost an afterthought, it seemed to Alex. "I'm sorry. I am, really."

She looked it, right enough. She had brought them down there, after all, Alex's look said. She held a hand up to counter his voicing this. He held his own up in turn. He had come of his own accord, after all. And her speech had conjured up those bored astronauts and almost made him laugh. She put a hand on his shoulder, and he said, "Sure – I know."

Indo appeared next to them.

"Everything good?" he asked, and they laughed, and explained their uninvited guest, though it was not a time for the ins and outs of the story. Indo took their word that it was worth laughing about. They followed him now along the paths and past the blocks, the shrubs and palms, black until the automatic lights came on to light their way. German voices sounded from the odd balcony, gruff, light-hearted, or gentle murmurs they only heard because they were passing close by, but the place really had put itself to bed in the half hour since Indo had finished his show.

They joined the hush, therefore, and spoke quietly about not much, where the bar was, which direction, how Indo had seen it from his car many times. They came out a gate and onto a quiet road.

"So, I guess your other... guests didn't want to come?" Indo asked.

Nuria was about to make some excuse but Alex almost snorted, said, "Not a chance." He laughed at the idea of Javier being anywhere near a jam session, imagined the look on his face, incredulous that people would spend time doing such a thing. He was fairly incredulous himself, he had to admit.

"Well, never mind. You will enjoy it, I hope."

It would be okay, Alex supposed. Nuria had simplified everything for him; his disappointment was indeed ridiculous. But Javier would not deign to stay in the staff dorm, of course. He would find a hotel. Maria would stay with him. How could Alex not be disappointed at the thought of it? *Don't think about it, then*, he imagined Nuria saying.

He and Nuria would have the staff dormitory to themselves. Alex was not sure if he ever thought the words out in that order. It was more like having a photo of the room flash into his mind every once in a while.

Some people would rather be doing anything but standing in front of Hieronymus Bosch's apocalyptic painting The Garden of Earthly Delights in Madrid's Prado. On the other hand, some people would like to be in it.

They walked up a road lined with holiday apartments, past their lush gardens and under their tall palm trees.

Most of the people in them seemed to have gone to bed, although there was the occasional group on a balcony, lit by candles whose flames were filtered red and green through wine bottles. It was quiet: no passers-by and hardly any cars. Alex liked the quiet, in theory, but knew he had done the right thing in opting to stay in Madrid to work.

Indo was a good listener, Alex thought, and a good talker too. He seemed aware that he and Nuria would be boring Alex whenever they dwelt on their shared experiences, so knocked those conversations on the head after a minute or so. He did this to the extent that Alex was still barely aware of the nature of Nuria's connection to him.

Indo got a phone call and hung back, chatting away hurriedly.

Alex had a sudden wish to go home. He could sneak past Señores, spend his free Sunday anonymously in Madrid, go to the Prado at last – he had never been. He imagined the paintings, the halls, the light, the people, the rustle of their guidebooks, the murmur of their voices, that gallery smell. He asked Nuria if she had ever been there, and she was puzzled by this irrelevant turn in the conversation.

"We could go there now," he said.

"Start walking, then," Nuria said, but sensed Alex's disappointment, and the source of it. "Maria and Javier are not loving," she told him. "They're just talking. It's a conversation they've had many times, and one that makes them both crazy. When it doesn't go his way, he'll be mean to her. He'll dump her at the bus station in Chiclana or Cádiz and make her get the bus. He's done it before." Bus stations, she recited, train stations, deserted service stops, small towns with no taxis: the middle of the night, a call from Maria, tears, a request sometimes impossible to answer – can Nuria get in her comic yellow car and come and get her, just a few hundred kilometres, or failing that get on her computer and look up a cab service or a cheap room?

"You know what? They just have to realise that they don't want to have that conversation again. Then it will end forever, but not till they realise that. But listen, Alex, if you really want to go, I can take you to Cádiz – but I don't think there's a bus at this time of night. If you *really* want to escape, Cádiz bus station is as good a place as any." She laughed. "You might even meet Maria there."

Alex bristled at the laughter. He sensed a little meanness in it, which perhaps prompted him into his own, and the words, "Maria's got two men fighting over her. I don't suppose that ever happens to you."

"*Hey.*" Nuria took a look at Alex, wondered if she ought to be offended. She decided to laugh it off, said, "I'm only attracted to pacifists, and to people who are fucking... *sensible.*"

They seemed to be walking an awfully long way to Alex, until, at last, they came upon a strip of ice cream bars, small cafés and restaurants – nearly all closed or closing – and there was its bright spot, the Saint Patrick's Tavern, where Nuria had stopped earlier to get her Irish directions.

It's a hard egg.

Alex was probably the most Irish thing in it. There was a small, convivial crowd of locals, he would learn, both expat Brits and Spaniards, plus a few end-of-season holidaymakers.

Indo was greeted like an old friend by several men there; handshakes and introductions were made. Within five minutes Alex thought he had at least nodded to most of the people present, and, within ten minutes, forgotten their names.

People went up to an area at the side of the bar and sang and played. A serious-looking long-haired bloke had a serious-looking guitar setup with lots of effects, most of them a bit much for a jam session, Alex thought, though they worked quite well when he did a rousing version of Stevie Wonder's *Superstition*. A kid that looked about twelve played both the guitar and a keyboard. He sang *Bye Bye Miss American Pie*, but mostly accompanied other people. Indo joined in as and when he was invited, but he seemed happy to tap his feet and listen and add to the applause.

An expat got up to sing *It's a Hard Egg*. Her matching skirt and shirt reminded Alex of the curtain clothes in *The Sound of Music*. He would not have been surprised to find a drawstring hanging from one sleeve. Alex stared at her for a long time, wondering if she was the original singer of the song, retired now and hiding out on the Costa de la Luz; she had the coughy voice exactly like the original, but perhaps she was just an everyday expat who, like most of the Brits in Spain, took advantage of the cheap tobacco and smoked too much.

In the Saint Patrick's Tavern, the Spaniards caught up with one another and sipped at their drinks. The Brits knocked them back with gusto and tried to outtalk one another, one group intent on telling every last detail of how difficult it was to get a conservatory built, another in and out of the verge of an argument, when one man insisted on calling another's Filipina wife *Losemaly* rather than, presumably, Rosemary. They were all crass. Alex was glad he was apart from them. He followed them only with his drinking. Nuria and Indo were drinking the same glass of wine for an hour, so Alex gave up gave up offering them drinks and just bought his lonely round of one.

He knew he was drunk when he found himself obsessed with finding out the name of the original *Hard Egg* singer and yet, whenever he was about to ask Indo, he was distracted by something else just as trivial, and forgot the question. He got Indo's attention with a raised finger, and said, "You know…"

"What, Alex?" Indo laughed, somewhat doubtfully.

Alex pointed at Indo's wooden cross and said, "Just like the original."

He was not drunk enough to accept an invitation to sing, thankfully.

Alex could not sing, or at least he could, if singing was making a noise with the vocal cords, but he did not for one moment believe that anybody would want to listen to him. He would have been like the Brit tourists who let their toddlers loose on the karaoke machines in the resorts; he had heard horror stories of them clearing bars in seconds flat. Indo made his last contribution with a Spanish tune and then a droning Oasis singalong. Alex was surprised to hear the Spaniards singing along with it as well as the Brits.

Alex thought about sharing the dorm room with Nuria. He drank some more. He was not exactly doing it on purpose. Or perhaps he was, the thought kept glowing. She yawned and reminded Alex of a lioness for a second. He put his hand over her mouth to hide the yawn and she laughed but was also puzzled; it was both comical and throwaway and yet also somehow intimate. Alex made it entirely comical by saying, "I wouldn't do that if you were vomiting."

She said, "I don't think I'll be the one vomiting tonight, Alex."

Maybe he would sing after all, he remembered thinking, the next day, but luckily got no further with it.

"*You* sing, Nuria," he remembered saying. "Yeah, a love song – sing us a *lurve* song." And she had looked at him, perplexed for a second: too loud, he almost saw her thinking, too repetitive, too slurred. "A *luuuuuuurve* song." She had looked closely then understood the state to which the booze had brought Alex's mind. "One of those... old-fashioned..." He reached the impasse of a look that said *sorry-what-were-we-talking-about-again-remind-me*?

Nuria threw her head back and laughed and said, "The music's finished. They're packing up – look." But all the same, she transformed her empty bottle into a microphone and sang softly just to him *Georgia on My Mind*... or was it *Midnight Train to Georgia*. Or *Sweet Georgia Brown*... Alex did not really know any of those songs, but deep in his mind was planted the name Georgia, a place that people wrote songs about – or were all the Georgias in the songs actually women?

He remembered saying to one of the Brits, "But you *do* know there's an English *town*, an *actual English town*, and this is no word of a *lie*, called Pawking le Walnut?" That was how it came back to him, amusing spelling and all, albeit lost in the utterance of it, although none of it was funny anyway. He also swore that *una paloma blanca* was Cockney rhyming slang from Newcastle.

"They don't speak it on this coast," he told somebody solemnly. "No Cockneys to speak it to, you see." He remembered looking around, left, right, and hunching conspiratorially, assuring his listeners, "I know you're all undercover Cockneys. Your secret is *literally* safe with me."

He sensed Nuria and Indo exchanging glances, remembered people saying goodnight, some of them looking at him with broad smiles, and the *Hard Egg* woman saying, "One's a crowd with him around," and Alex looking around to see who she meant. He yelled, "Thank you for the music," in English and Spanish. He was apologising for not knowing how to say it in Swedish, just like Abba, as he was guided into the back of a cab, saw the dancing lights on the deserted road, and was taken back to the dorm at the Sol.

'Make me feel real loose, like a long-necked goose

Like a girl, oh baby, that's what I like.'
Chantilly Lace, Jiles Perry

Alex woke up drunk and woozy, not knowing, for a minute, where he was. Nuria was snoring on a bed near his.

He got up, threw up in the loo then went out onto the balcony for some air. He saw a small group of people walking along one of the paths through the trees, at ease and talking quietly, oblivious to his gaze. One of the men was carrying what looked like a freshly-killed bird, a swan, a goose, perhaps – massive, its long neck hanging down, head swinging gently. It could have been dry cleaning, Alex had to admit, eventually. But at mad o'clock in the morning when people were drunk and had had their entire lives ruined, they were allowed to be fanciful. He watched out for people singing a song about Walter Gropius, whoever he was, and in German, and wondered whether the mysterious Walter had sung *It's a Hard Egg*. He knew that he was confused and yet was able to think lucidly that he was confused so, therefore, could not have been *too* confused. It was cold out there. As his eyes closed, he knew he should have been somewhere else – was it the Prado, back in Madrid? Probably not. He went back into the room. The bed he had been sleeping in looked impossibly far away. He fell onto the nearest one and slept.

~

"I like sitting by the sea."
"Why?"
"What? Why *why? Do you need a reason?"*
"Yeah."
"You don't like the sea?"
"It's okay."
"Okay? It's fucking... elemental, *is the sea."*
"Isn't that a cheese?"

Nuria made Alex get up and suggested he be sick again, said it would be a good idea if he showered too and got into clean clothes. She made him pack and led him out past the reception desk, where she placed the key.

"Where are we going?" he asked, and warned, "I can't do breakfast."

She did not care, she said. He looked at her spare frame and wondered, as he often did, if she ever ate anything ever.

"Just come with me," she said, so he did. As they entered the car park, she said, "Where's my car?"

Alex pointed. "The yellow one – look."

"Ha – the *yellow* one. Do you see?"

"What?"

"In the middle of all the grey and black and silver? Another good reason to have a yellow car."

They stowed their bags in the boot and then Nuria led him along a dusty path past a forlorn-looking shopping centre, shut now till the season resumed, and then along wooden walkways amid scrub and sand.

"Not far now," she said, whenever he seemed to be dawdling.

"What's not far?"

"The sea, of course."

Of course – Alex knew that, really. The dust-laden bushes fell away to reveal the Costa de la Luz – the Coast of Light, and indeed it had a big bright sky, only slightly moody, casting its shade on the day. Alex liked the look of it at once.

Nuria led him down the walkway and onto the sand. She stopped to unlace her shoes and pull them off, and Alex did the same.

There were plenty of people around, but the beach was too vast to be crowded. Alex had never seen a beach like it; it stretched away in both directions for miles, the people walking along it disappearing into a haze of heat and spray from the lively waves that rolled in from the Atlantic. There were people on blankets and towels, playing with beach balls, kids doing the mystifying work of sand excavation and construction, but mostly people strolled, fully dressed or wearing next-to-nothing, a non-stop promenade until they became stick-people, then ghosts, and vanished.

"Good beach?"

Alex felt himself under scrutiny. He said, "Fantastic."

"A two-hour walk." Nuria gestured right and left. "Each way."

"Really?"

"At least."

"That's a lot of beach."

Alex was disappointed when he realised that he was not going to get out into the water to swim. He had been going nuts back in Madrid for a sight of the sea, a smell of it, the feel of it; this was the Atlantic, though, and it was savage. The water was elemental, not calming, not a place for leisure, but to be vigilant – the sea was generally rather disquieting in its overall effect.

The waves looked deadly. There were people in the water, some in late-season wetsuits, but they were not swimming, were just being tossed around like debris. Alex wondered how often such people took a part in their own doom that way and perished. Their distant cries of excitement were disturbing: their raised hands signs of enjoyment or lack of control. Alex spied a man out a long way who kept appearing and disappearing. Distracted by something Nuria was saying, he took his eye off the man. The next time he looked, he was gone. He may have drowned or floated off to Brazil. Or both.

Alex forgot him. There was the journey back to preoccupy him, there was Maria to forget, and Javier to hate, there was the name of the woman who had sung *It's a Hard Egg* to rediscover, and all kinds of important things.

Nuria said, "You didn't have to get *so* drunk."

That was true. He could have pretended. He wondered if, like a lot of Spanish people, she just disapproved of drunkenness. It was not that, though; she was smart, knew that he had got drunk so that the subject of sleeping with her would not come up, and that, later, neither of them could be accused of trying to make it happen. The transparency of the ploy only hit home right then, and he was mortified for a second. He stopped. When Nuria stopped too and sent him a look of enquiry, he moved his shoulders, spread his hands, decided to forget it and invited her to do so too.

She said, "You were quite hilarious."

"Was I?" He thought about it. A remnant of the English teacher he had been prompted him to check, "Do you mean, like, a *bit* hilarious, or... *very* hilarious?"

"Very," she decided.

He was very hungover, anyway. Nuria saw that and dropped her questions. They walked.

Beaches were good for people-watching, Alex remembered. He was amazed, as ever, by the patience of the sunbathers, their ability to do nothing but lie in the sun of very late September for hours in the hope of getting burned just enough not to be alarmed. The idiot director of studies at the Cambridge College had used some fancy moisturiser on his face to combat the sun in Spain, a thing with a shocking price tag. And he still looked like a fucking roasted tomato. Alex had always thought such people were stupid, or at least easily pleased, but perhaps they led frantic and busy lives and adapted well to downtime and nothingness.

Deep down, Alex did not really approve of holidays. He thought it was pointless to go for the illusion of freedom and happiness for two weeks a year – three, four, what did it matter? It was the non-holidays that should have been the happy times.

One woman sat up and ate. She was proof that no matter how tanned, cool or pretty a woman could be, there was no way to eat a ripe peach without looking like a cat savaging a rodent. Alex caught Nuria's eye; she had seen the same thing. They laughed and Nuria punched Alex lightly on the shoulder and said, "Don't read my mind, Alex."

"I will if I want."

"You may not like everything in there. Listen." She stopped looking at him and scanned the distance, the sand, the holiday homes bordering the beach. She beckoned him to sit down. "Maria doesn't have a bucket list. She has a fuck-it list. She will fuck anybody."

But not me, Alex thought.

"But not you." Nuria took her turn to read his mind.

"Why?" He felt in thrall to her scrutiny.

"Alex, I don't know for sure. And I don't think my answer will please you, but I think it's because she thinks you're too nice. No, listen. Really, honestly, I think if you were more... aggressive about it she'd respond differently."

"I can't do that," Alex said.

"No. I know. You're western, and middle class."

"I'm not middle *class*." It was an occasional sore point with Alex. The son of a barman and an academic, a secondary-modern-educated black north Londoner and a private-schooled Dublin Southsider with what was called an *independent* income as well as a lucrative career, Alex did not really believe in class. He thought the notion of it had been eradicated. He tended to agree that there were the rich, and the underclass, and the people in the middle of them. The discussion usually ended when somebody pointed out that those people – "You know, Alex, the ones in the fucking *middle*?" – *were* the middle class, and that Alex, being neither rich nor a chav, was definitely one of them, whether he wanted to be or not.

"I told you it wouldn't please you. Well then, what, I don't know – *educated*, then," Nuria said. "Whatever. Maria thinks that western women have been so successful in frightening western men that this will finally, one day long after we are all dead, of course, be the end of western civilisation, because all the men will be either gay or sterile or have dicks the size of lentils."

"I'm not middle class," Alex tried to insist. "But I'm not a caveman, either."

"And who *is*?"

"What?"

"Who *is* a caveman, Alex, that you know?"

"Javier." Alex had been about to pretend he didn't know what Nuria was talking about, but he knew he could hardly keep it up if he wanted to discuss it. Nuria greeted the name with a triumphant, exaggerated movement of her lips. It was all there in that name, a complex story from which Alex was always going to be excluded.

"Javier." The mention of the name was an attempt at dismissal. Nuria changed the subject with her finger and pointed at a family sat around their towels: a man, a woman, two girls of about three or four, who were alike enough to be twins.

She said, "It's all jolly now."

"*Jolly*," he repeated, a little scornfully, though he enjoyed Nuria's occasional use of some word long out of currency.

"*Jolly*," she insisted. "Wait till they're fourteen, though."

"And pregnant," he sort of agreed.

"Exactly. *Yes*. And mixed up with South American drug cartels."

Alex's getting the joke and joining in with it lifted their spirits a little.

"My dick's not the size of a lentil," he thought he ought to establish.

They walked on. Nuria signalled Alex to stop, and sat down, fanned herself and pulled her fleece off. It may have been nearly the end of September, but it was still in the low twenties. Alex had looked up the weather in advance and been prudent, brought a pair of those dreadful knee-off shorts his dad had liked, and which Alex associated with old geezers on holiday, or pole-propelled trekking Germans.

Nuria stood up suddenly, unzipped her jeans and wriggled them down.

"Hot," she said, and, when she saw him scanning her long, skinny legs, her dark blue knickers, said, "Don't look."

"I'm not." He turned away. Nobody looked on beaches, and yet, Alex suspected, everybody did.

Nuria's phone chimed, and she pulled it out of her pocket and looked at it, said, "Maria," and ignored it. "She can leave a message," she explained to Alex. "I am so... pissed off with her, Alex. *Alex*," she said urgently, "*don't* love her. Really. Don't. Only a fucking... *idiot* would love her. She's my friend, and I'd do almost anything for her, but I don't *love* her." She wrinkled her nose and touched Alex under the chin as if he were a child or a pet. "Nobody can *love* her. Even her parents don't love her."

The phone went again, and this time Nuria hesitated then relented and answered. Alex gathered that Maria was on the beach somewhere, with Javier of course, and would be going back to Madrid with him in his lovely new car. Of course.

"Well, that's a surprise," Alex heard Nuria say, then heard her explaining, "Yes, girlfriend, I fucking *am* being sarcastic," before she closed off the call.

Alex realised that none of it mattered. He could have had all the time in the world to schmooze Maria and entice her away from Javier, could even have fucked her, if he could find his caveman within, but it just did not matter: she was in Javier's thrall and would never consider Alex as a partner as long as she was there, no matter the circumstances. It was just one of those things. Paradoxically, he was almost happy to see this so clearly; it framed his lack of success neatly. What could he ever have done against one of nature's done deeds?

Nuria shook her head at Alex and said, "I'm sorry, Alex, but you really are better off without her. She will carry on hurting him, will drive him insane – if that's a... consolation to you. I don't think so. I don't think you are so mean. But she's hell on legs, Alex – really. I know you don't believe me, but she is. Javier is... probably not a bad man. He is a simple man. He doesn't try to be sophisticated, and he doesn't understand people who are. And sometimes that makes him appear to be stupid, and brutish. He works, makes money and wants a wife to make babies. What he sees in Maria to make him think *she* fits into this, I really, really...

really don't know. My main fear sometimes is that he'll kill her, but then..."

"What?" Alex was not sure how seriously to take Nuria's alarming claim.

"Then I look at them together and it's *so* clear that she'll be the one to survive."

"*Yeah.*" It seemed crystal clear to Alex too. He had no idea why.

This gloomy thought in mind, they got up. Both had been fixated for a few minutes on the sun-splashed flag above the Sol that guided its guests back for their dinner and seat-saving, their mystifying bilingual songs in the night and their gentle drinking and dancing. It was tiny and far away. They looked at their watches and the thought of the road and the need to go home, and turned and traipsed back along the beach, marvelling at it all over again.

As they walked back through the closed-down buildings over the beach, the sight prompted melancholy in Alex. Some places were open, some closed, some on the verge. They were like the last half-hour at the Señores bar; it was only for a few saddos who just could not face going home. Alex served them not as part of the convivial time he was supposed to be providing, but as part of some stupid ritual devoid of meaning. A half-asleep resort was a bit like that. He was glad he worked in Madrid where nothing closed, hot or cold weather, high or low season, with tourists present or not – it was life, compared to the yearly death suffered by towns like Novo Sancti Petri. He got into Nuria's car and let her steer him away from death and from failure, and from the rain that had started to come down as they walked across the car park.

FOUR

The rain in Spain. It never stays on the plain. It rushes down those crusty river valleys loosening tons of yellow clay and makes it liquid, under those bridges you thought were pointless. It's something to see, a rare sight, even as it ruins your holiday for you. You can get rain back in England. But not like this, not like this.

The rain looked like a tease for a while but then fell hard, emptied the streets of Novo Sancti Petri and blotted out the last few roundabouts into Chiclana. After the dry spell, the road became slippery. Even so, a driver behind Nuria beeped his horn. She ordered Alex, "Give him the finger." He resisted the temptation.

He had gone past annoyance, which had its own energy, and was dispirited. Even with the thought that his failure with Maria had been mitigated by the elemental force in which he was caught between her and Javier, it still made him feel that a depression was coming on. Alex's mum had almost convinced him that depression was a thing you wished upon yourself, an extreme form of self-pity.

Though he did not entirely agree, he had developed various strategies for dealing with it that involved a little positive thinking, some self-delusion and some alcohol, but the thing that really banished it was work. He was glad to be heading back to the Señores bar that evening. He would do the stores and prepare the paperwork for the week ahead and it would take him much of the night. He would work the bar and collect glasses and wipe tables and have a friendly, obvious word for all the customers, perhaps even a laugh, and he would get lost in it and forget his weekend on the Costa de la Luz, forget the place forever until it called him back in a happier state.

Nuria talked about work, a little, talked about the rain, a little, a sign of the coming winter, she reminded Alex. She talked about the way the season affected her, brought her a gloom that was a challenge to face, but mostly she concentrated on her driving, relaxing when the rain eased off and the sun came out again.

"Last chance to eat for a while," she said, nodding at a fast-food joint as she followed the road out of Chiclana. "Or are you never going to eat again?"

"Something like that." Alex had not thought about food, it was true. Nuria said no more, put her foot down and headed down a ramp onto the motorway, sped out onto it, pointed Alex to the satnav, and gave him the job of seeking out the signs.

Nothing but a hard egg.

Both were content with silence. Anything Nuria said was not going to help Alex avoid his mood, and it was good that they could both acknowledge that. He looked out on the haze made by rain and cars, the road and its markings that merged into a blur as the car collected them into its slipstream, and the roadsides that bled into the brightening sky. Alex kept telling himself that he would be home in a matter of hours, grounded again, his thoughts aimed only on the small cross-section of the world that congregated at Señores.

Nuria had not bothered to ask for a description of Javier's new car the evening before, and Alex would have been hard pushed to remember it. All the same, he knew it when he saw it; it was part of a tableau on the hard shoulder ahead, coming rapidly into focus as Nuria approached it. The other familiar element in it was the figure of Maria Betancur.

"They've broken down." Alex could not resist the crow of triumph that drifted into his voice. His spirits flagged, then rallied, when he realised that Javier would have to wait there to have the car repaired or removed, but that Maria was hardly going to stand on the hard shoulder for hours; she would be coming back to Madrid with them. Then he remembered that he was done with her and would be ignoring her, or doing the neutral thing he was never very good at, which nearly always became clumsily passive-aggressive and made him cringe not only later, but during its enactment. His spirits dipped again.

Alex could see Nuria fighting a dilemma and sensed that she could quite happily have left Maria there. She cursed and slowed down.

As they slowed, the picture changed. Javier was in the car, revving the engine. Maria was picking stuff up, a range of clothes – far too many, Alex could see at once, for a night by the sea – make-up and tan lotion, a paperback, a magazine, bathing costumes, towels, a fucking alarm clock in a child's bright pink. A shimmery evening dress over her shoulder, she was trying, with some difficulty, to fit it all into a torn rucksack. Alex saw the slapstick in it; she put one thing in, which dislodged another and then both fell out, and she cursed and started again. It seemed plain that her bag had been thrown down with some force.

Alex got out of the car and called over to Javier to ask what was going on. He received a *fuck-off* in return. Alex stood by Javier's window and bit his lip. As he had done the evening before, he was considering punching him. What kind of man could make a peace-loving guy like Alex fall to such rage? A caveman, of course. Nuria said nothing to Maria, just joined her in picking up items and putting them into her boot. Maria set off on a tearful rant. Alex did not need to listen to it.

"You're *so* classy," he said to Javier. "I'm not going to lie to you, but I was puzzled as to why Maria... *appreciated* you so much – in fact, I was mystified. But now I know. You are fucking... *special*."

"I don't want your opinion," Javier said. "Go and serve your drinks."

"*Motherfucker!*" The word was not a feature of Alex's vocabulary. He was shocked, later, to recall hearing himself use it in anything other than an ironic sense. He was not really aiming the word at Javier, either, just expressing his exasperation with the whole weekend. Javier had not wound the window up; it was plain to Alex that he was, almost, indifferent to the idea that Alex might punch him. That put Alex on his guard; whether it was so Javier could get out and legitimately beat the shit out of him or call the law on him, Alex did not know – the latter, he suspected. Alex had got fighting over a girl once before. He had also been beaten up because of the colour of his skin, and also because he had wandered into the wrong late-night street full of drunks. He was acutely aware of the consequences of impromptu fisticuffs but sensed that twatting Javier one would have led him into something long-running and tedious. He forced himself into a smile and saw it register in Javier's face as a flush of anger beneath his tanned skin.

Alex turned, happy to have conquered this moment of potential violence, and called to Nuria and Maria, "Hey, should I do some *retrieving*, too?"

He stopped, clicked fingers, said, "Bonnie Tyler."

That got everybody's attention, even Javier's, who narrowed his glare a touch.

Nuria said, "The singer?" She looked around. "Where?"

"Sang *It's a Hard Egg.*" Alex felt pleased to have remembered.

Maria straightened up and wiped a tear away. She looked puzzled but noted, "And that other one," as she made a last sweep of the ground for the remainder of her possessions. "The one with the..." She swept a hand up, trying to think of a prompt, Alex guessed, a scene in a video, some musical phrase.

Javier revved some more. He put his head out of the side window and told Nuria to fuck off out of his way. She made no reply, simply stood in front of the car. She reached out, took the aerial in her hand and tried to snap it. She pulled at it, but it was nylon, and well fixed. She banged at it with a gesture of disgust, and at least got the satisfaction of bending it out of shape; it looked like a Dali squiggle, the one Alex had seen claimed for the artist in an optimistic dealer's portfolio. She nodded to herself and moved out of the way, swept her arm up to tell Javier to go and shouted things at him that Alex could not make out, though he could guess their purpose. Maria had a good old shout too as she got into the rear of Nuria's car. Javier seemed content to rev. He looked to Alex as if he were considering getting out of the car. He said something to Nuria that Alex could not catch. On the point of getting into the back with Maria, Alex paused, but Nuria was walking. She walked round to the back of Javier's car and popped open the boot. Only then did she seem satisfied.

Javier's car looked different in the daylight. It had never been remarkable, and after a schlep through the rain, it looked shinier, but still less than new. It was just some car. It was fancy enough to have a button to press to close the boot, Alex supposed, but Javier had not yet sussed out where it was. They watched him get out with a curse and followed him with their eyes as he made impatient strides to go and close it manually.

Nuria was white-faced and angry and yet, Alex remembered later, the anger stayed concentrated in her face. Her movements as she opened the door, sat back in the seat, fastened her seatbelt and started the engine, put it in first and got it to bite, were all precise and measured; her gear changes as they got going were smooth and almost silent. She trundled along the hard shoulder and scooted them onto the road.

She called back to Maria and Alex, "Fasten your fucking seatbelts, please," and Alex at least managed to smile as the car raced them back into the mist and the rain, the stream of vehicles and lives, the sky meeting the land to confuse and reassure them at the same time.

When your wishes take to the air in flying metal and upholstery, broken plastic – wiring, chrome-coated countersunk screws, an abandoned polystyrene coffee cup with a name scrawled on it... when your wishes will draw a forensics team... the writer of an obituary... when they make your frustration manifest and give it teeth and deeds – what then? Happiness?

They were on the verge of talk, perhaps even of a tentative laugh, when Nuria raised her chin to her rear-view mirror and said, "Look," as softly as she could. "*Behind* us." She addressed their puzzlement, their forward gazes. Alex and Maria turned. Out the back window they could see that Javier was coming fast at them in his bargain, skipping past cars without indicating. A horn sounded, then became a trio of horns and then a quintet, because drivers loved a play on their horns, until it went from vindictive fun to impatience to terror in a squawking symphony.

Nuria, Alex and Maria watched, fascinated, silenced, though none of them saw exactly what happened as those horns came together in a crescendo. Javier's car hit another car, or another car hit Javier's and then another and possibly even another, or more, at a hundred kilometres an hour or more. There were screeches from car tyres and metal and, perhaps, voices, then a series of loud bangs, glimpses of frightened faces, cars absurdly facing the wrong way, a crunch of glass and metal, and the impression of car parts going through the air.

They were separated from it by three or four cars, no more, two road-marked chevrons, Alex thought he recalled, but it was enough for them to escape the impacts and the shock waves. Nuria carried on, and it was plain that she was not heading for the hard shoulder to stop.

"Hey, hang on," Alex said.

Nuria did not even acknowledge him.

"Hold up," he said, watching the shrinking scene out the back window. "What, drive on – let him burn? Is that it?"

"Burn?" Nuria said. "Oh, fuck *off*, Alexander. You watch too many films. *Let him* burn," she quoted scornfully. "Let his shirt be slightly creased, more like."

Maria said, "Yeah. Let his wafer-thin watch lose a few seconds."

Alex looked from one to the other. *Cold*, he thought – callous. He felt like a child in thrall to adult mischief, like in a Victorian story, not quite understanding what was going on.

He remembered his wish the previous evening in Chiclana that Javier should crash. He suffered a pang of guilt but was not superstitious enough to dwell on it. He remembered clearly that his wish had been for a bit of a prang – he remembered imagining Javier stepping out of the car to inspect the damage, watching the steam come out of the radiator, like in some slapstick old black-and-white film – and the crash caused by a careless moment, and not by Javier's ego and hubris.

The banal truth was, he saw now, was that Javier's car was a crock. The non-locking boot was a clue; the electrics were slow, was Alex's layman guess, as an observer of other people's car troubles. He remembered more than a few lights on Javier's dash blinking in distress. Not hired only to gentle septuagenarians for trundles to the shops, then, but perhaps to maniacs who boy-raced it along the coast at two hundred kilometres per hour, caned it to Tarifa, then Gibraltar, Algeciras, blagged their way over to Tangier and pitted it against sand and date pits and camel shit and wrecked it. Who knew?

And in such an ill-used tin can, what the *actual fuck* could Javier have been thinking of – what, some insult he had just been unable to keep for another time? *And another thing...* Had he not heard of texting? That was dangerous enough in itself while driving... Alex guessed they would never know. He gazed at Maria in a kind of wonder. Sheer rage had made Javier drive in such a way, surely – he had certainly not been trying to catch them up to apologise. He gazed, and Maria gazed back. She poked her tongue out at him and grinned. He marvelled at her power, getting men to make such eager fools of themselves. He was among them, of course; acknowledging this was the beginning of his release.

For her own benefit as well as Alex's, he thought later, Nuria recited the logistical difficulties involved in stopping and turning around and pointed out that by the time they found an exit to take them back, the emergency services would be there, the slip road would be closed, the traffic at a standstill.

All true, all logical, but it was still cold. It was not just Maria – both of them were trouble. He felt that he was out of his depth, and it was a little shocking, a little dismaying, and he shook his head.

As the cars ahead of them picked up speed, Nuria slowed down to such an extent that they had the road near-enough to themselves until the next exit. They heard sirens and, in the opposite lane, saw emergency vehicles heading back the way they had come.

"We weren't witnesses," Nuria said, a few kilometres on. "We didn't see what happened, did we? What *actually* happened? Well, *did* we?" It was true. Maria remained silent, looking out the window; she did not seem to have an opinion on their decision to drive on. Even Alex was not sure how he really felt about it. But yes, there were, no doubt, better witnesses than them. Anything they could have said would have simply added to Javier's trouble. If he was alive.

It was still wrong, though – well, still not *right*, at least.

Alex said, "He might be dead." He had once seen the aftermath of a road accident, his cab home from a late-night thing at work brought to a crawl on a street on the edge of Newcastle: all police and paramedics and their lights and gear and, on the road, the wreckage of a motorbike and parts of two cars strewn along for a shockingly long way, startled and dazed faces white in the lights. That had been like a snapshot. The grotesque enactment he had just seen had burst through the screen of the rain into hideous colour, sound and movement. "Have you thought of that?"

Maria got her phone out, pulled a number and pressed it and declared, "Voicemail." She grinned, said, "Hey, what message shall I leave the foolish man... Oops!" That became the message.

Nuria looked at Alex, her lips pursed, to let him know she had a message for Javier for sure, but that it could keep. She caught Maria's eyes in the mirror and snapped, "*Not* funny." To Alex's surprise, Maria agreed and seemed to apologise, though neither agreement nor apology made it into words – it showed in her face, Alex thought.

"My name's not Alexander." It was something with which to break the silence as they drove on, the road, the sky, the day, back to their relentless, dull pace. He was not even sure if he wanted to break it. He was afraid, he realised as soon as he spoke, of what might replace it.

Maria said, "No – really? What is it, then?"

"It's just *Alex*. I mean..." His translation got him saying, "My *official* name."

Nuria said, "I know."

"Eh?" he said. "How?"

She said, "I looked at your passport while you were asleep."

"What – why?"

"I don't know."

Alex looked at Maria, but her expression seemed to support Nuria's; sneaking a look at somebody's passport photo was the most natural thing in the world.

"I can call you Alexander," Maria said. "If you like."

"I don't." Alex shook his head in mock-disbelief then remembered with a jolt that he too once had examined a friend's passport photo when they were not looking... in fact twice, two different friends.

"New identity – Alexander." Maria said. "Ah *yih*!"

Alex noted the expression almost in passing and got as far as halfway through a perfunctory nod. Maria had delivered a fair rendition of one of Math Bookbinder's favourite expressions. At the same time, he noted that Nuria was busy trying to catch Maria's eyes in hers in the mirror. Maria did not see it.

"Ah-*yih*," Alex echoed, neutrally. He had never been able to work out whether the boyish affirmative was genuine New Zealand, or just Math sending up Aussies. He felt like some stern uncle, when he said, "So where did you learn that from, then?" The question was ridiculous.

"Isn't it Australian?" Maria looked puzzled. She and a reluctant Nuria had a quick discussion about it. "Kiwi?" she asked Nuria. "Like the little fruit? Kiwi," she affirmed, for Alex.

Nuria kept her eyes on the road and her lips clamped shut.

"From my... friend." Maria made the word linger, pouted, looked away and waved Math away. There was something about the way she said it that was both coy and knowing.

Alex thought about Math, and also waved him away. There were a few questions on his lips, but he scrunched them into the side of his Picasso face.

Without looking at her, Nuria said to Maria, "Well *done*."

Maria said, "What?"

"Fucking... out*standing*."

"*What?*"

It was the last word spoken for some time. The silence afforded Alex the time to think about Maria and her New Zealand friend – their mutual friend, of course. Alex remembered Nuria telling him that Maria had fucked somebody at the school and his assumption that it was a student. He remembered his scrutiny of Maria's fellow-students when they had come into Señores – not obsessive, nor even obtrusive, and they would not have suspected a thing as he served them their drinks and tapas, but all the same he had done it. How *foolish*. Had Math known that Alex had a thing for Maria? He had mentioned it to Math for sure, his hots for a friend of Nuria's. But so what?

Somewhere near Seville, Alex realised that if nothing else had come of the weekend, he was free of Maria Betancur; she really had cured him of her. It did not mean they would not be friends – it was, frankly, fucking unlikely – but for sure he could reset his life to a time before he gave a toss about her.

He shut his eyes and saw Javier's car levitating – what was it, again? Who cared? Just some *car...* doing a flip on the motorway, the same drama as a pinball gathering momentum as it flew off the obstacles, spectacular for a second or two. Then scrap metal. Where was Javier's vanity now? Where was his bargain? *Scrap fucking metal.* Fuck *him.* And yet Alex was still slightly perturbed at their not having stopped. He knew that he would justify it in any of a few ways; of course, Alex did not like him, and nor did Nuria. But Maria was supposed to love him, and even she had not urged them to stop. When he got the time to think about it, Javier was surely going to reach the same conclusion as Alex: he too would learn to live without Maria – *surely.*

Alex would have gone back, he told himself – easier said than done, he knew, but not impossible – he would have tried, anyway. Nuria and Maria were a pair of black widows, he thought, and his overall feeling as they joined the Sunday afternoon queues on roads that had not been subject to accidents, that day, was that of feeling trapped.

Soon, the absence becomes its own presence, wounds heal and close and are forgotten, and the body is all the better for it. And you can drink yourself silly, too, as a bonus. (Folksy proverb claimed or denied by any and all nations)

Alex forgot her. For a time he saw her everywhere: a five-year-old boy who was going to grow up to look like Maria Betancur, and a seventy-five-year old woman, who'd grown old and graceful out of looking like Maria Betancur, the child oblivious, the pensioner amused, wondering perhaps if she'd left a grain of yellow rice at the corner of her mouth... an actress in a soap, a softball player on TV, a guard on the Metro, all looking like Maria Betancur.

But really, what had she ever been to Alex? Something destined to be unattainable. Nuria was surely right; perhaps if he had tried a little harder, he could have had her body for a while, at least. He had wanted her heart instead, though, her soul – well, all right, her mind, then, all its landscapes, and memories, all its attention. Had that been too much to ask? Obviously, it had – of course it had.

"Why?" Nuria asked him, several times. She was never able to hide her amusement. Alex thought she fancied herself as Aphrodite – perhaps it was a complex, written about in psychiatric studies – helping men lose their hearts, then laughing at the results, sadly but self-indulgently, saying, "What lovelorn fools these men are, wasting their limited mortality in such a way." Alex pretended to Nuria that he could not put the why into words – a double bluff, as it was true.

"You can't have *any*body's mind, Alex."

He had to agree, though he never sounded convinced. And he had had to ask Nuria, "Did you know about Math?" He remembered his friend coming into Señores, looking uncharacteristically apologetic; he was going away the next day, of course. Alex had very mixed feelings. He was not even sure he had discussed Maria with Math in any detail; he had probably played it down. And in any case, Math fucking Maria was only a small part of Alex's malaise.

"Do you want me to tell you?" Nuria said.

"Yeah." Alex held a hand up. "No."

"Well, then. Yeah, then. And no. What does it matter, Alex? She's the same as ever." She reminded him that Maria wasn't some pocket goddess, was just her flaky friend. She sometimes reminded him too that Maria was not just out there *some*where; she was near, passed the Señores bar often, stopped outside once, to call Nuria. It was a warning, Alex supposed. Alex did not mind hearing about Maria. It rubbed away the mystery and the gloss, left him wondering what the fuss had been about.

"You're one of those men I've read about." Nuria wagged a finger. "Who only goes after women who don't want them, so that they can justify their misogyny."

Alex was outraged, went to grab his coat and bag and leave, spluttered out, "I can't believe you said that. I can't believe you think it."

"I don't," she said brightly. "I'm just bored with the whole subject. She's my friend – okay, sure – but I would quite like never to mention the bitch again."

Alex was half-cheered and half-disappointed, though not as much as the people who had wanted their table in Il Morto Che Parla, and had twitched into life to make a move for it when they had seen Alex go for his bag and coat.

"I won't mention her again," Alex promised, and was able to keep it. He hardly ever saw Nuria anyway, and one day he went from feeling the absence of Maria around him in the city to the odd feeling that she had never existed outside his imagination.

FIVE

'Cultivate your staff. They are one of your prime assets, at least as important as the product you sell.' Alex's boring book on best-practice housekeeping in the hospitality business, highlighted. Well, fucking obviously: Alex's note in the margin. *The words* Jeffrey Dante *had been added then scribbled out.*

Alex stopped for a coffee one day in a new-style café with a silly name. As the *barista* – what was a fucking *barista* even *doing* in Spain? – cleared away his empty cup, she said, "I hope you enjoyed your coffee."

Alex looked up from his boring book on the role of best-practice housekeeping in the hospitality business. He had to stop himself saying, "Seriously?" The barista's slightly prominent chin made her look both defensive and aggressive, her sulky mouth barely hiding her teeth. If not actually that tall, her thinness made her look it. Her long dark hair was tied back in a careless bunch. It was clear to Alex that she did not care whether he had enjoyed his coffee or not. Why should she? It was a shame, Alex thought, that college students, and graduates too, had to abase themselves in such a way for a minimum-wage job with a foreign name – a proper shame. He wanted to give her a tip, but there was no... place for it. The drill was self-service, the polystyrene counter cup for tips an eyesore, an absurd cheek and an irrelevance to an old-school barman.

Alex was sometimes more like Jeffrey Dante than he imagined, and something about that got up his nose. It may have been then that he decided to stop being an old-school barman and go for the job that had been recommended to him – and, the hint went, for which he had been recommended – as bar manager at a swanky Cádiz hotel. In such a position, he could do something for the minimum-wagers who would work for him. He had no idea what but, for sure, were he in charge, he would absolve them from enquiring whether punters had enjoyed their drinks.

He gave the girl a tip anyway.

Alex liked the frank look that came into her dark eyes as she thanked him, a hint of interest, or perhaps curiosity. She tilted her head, nodded it imperceptibly. Alex liked the delicate leafy creeper tattooed on her wrist and disappearing into her sleeve, liked the piercing in her lower lip – again, like his dad, he had often disdained what he thought of as 'that *hey-I'm-so-tribal* kind of thing'.

Her name was Aida. She was a Madrileña. She was twenty-three and halfway through a degree in Fashion Design. Alex would soon have to field the question, "What, *Aida*, like in the opera?" Just as, all those years before, he had had to wait for a question about his own name to enable him to learn about it, the first enquiry got him puzzled. He had had to ask Aida, "Why didn't you tell me there was an opera called *Aida*?" He learned that, if he pre-empted people and said, "like in the opera," whoever he said it to would not have heard of Verdi's ancient Egypt slave-girl epic. He began to split people he met into those who had heard of *Aida* the opera and those who had not, as he told more and more people about his Aida and her studies in Madrid and her small, friendly family, her nice hair and dark eyes and bright teeth and dainty feet, the strange clothes she made and wore, and about her wit and charm and about the plans they were making together.

He got the hotel job and went to work in Cádiz. Aida had to stay in Madrid for her studies. They would survive it, they were both sure.

Apparition no.1: the ghost who reminded Alex of the Dali squiggle and its hidden riches.
"Seriously, Alex?"
"For sure."
"Ah-yih!"

There was a part of the hotel devoted to conferences, all neutral décor that was dull and sterile and on the verge of unfriendly and designed, certainly, to keep attendees' minds on their business. Alex stood and watched a crowd of delegates milling in the lobby, free for the day, the buffet in full swing. He heard a dry, mirthless laugh. He connected it at once to the back of Nuria Hidalgo's yellow Fiat the day of the trip to Novo Sancti Petri. He sought it out and immediately recognised a stocky figure whose face bore a livid scar squiggling up from his neck; another lost Dali.

Alex's first instinct was to head for his office – it was the way of least trouble. The idea that he should greet Javier Bonanno only trailed fleetingly through his mind. He went about his usual business: checked with the waitress in charge about staff and supplies, treated the head barman to much the same questions, nodded to any of the conference organisers he saw and left, did a round of the other bars, greeted the evening staff, and only then went to his office to go through his paperwork.

An hour later, Alex wandered out and swept an eye over the lobby's temporary bar and saw that it was cleared, linen in a pile and the trestle tables broken down. Most of the networkers had dispersed. Alex had checked the room registers and had seen that Javier was not staying in the hotel.

Across the lobby, Javier was talking to a small group – addressing them like a public meeting, Alex observed. Old habits die hard. He turned away to leave, then became aware of Javier's eyes on him.

He crossed the lobby, passed very close to Javier and his companions and went into the public loo. He would usually have used the hidden staff toilet. He washed his hands slowly and splashed his face. When he exited, Javier was waiting there, a metre and a half away. He had the poise of a bullfighter, Alex thought, his back straight, legs together but feet a little apart, chin slightly raised. If it was at all possible to do nothing pointedly, Javier Bonanno was doing it. As there was another loo in plain sight across the lobby, it was clear that Javier had stood on that spot to wait for Alex, but also that he was neither going to look at him nor acknowledge Alex's gesture of holding the door open for him. Alex had been snubbed better than that, though, and had snubbed others better. His one regret was that he never got the chance to ask Javier what he had thought he was doing, that day back on the motorway, but... fuck *him* anyway, for the last time – *double*-fuck him.

He thought back to that day and thought about Nuria Hidalgo and Maria Betancur – he had not thought about them for a while – and wondered where they were and what they were up to. But not for very long.

Apparition no.2: the ghost who smiled, and reminded Alex to keep listening.

Alex spent a long time on the road between Cádiz and Madrid. It was a long way after a week's work, but in any case, it was not possible to get back to Madrid every weekend. Aida had plenty of college work to do in her final year and often had to do her *barista* thing at the weekends. They were surviving it, Alex had to remind himself, more often than he liked.

On one such trip, back to Madrid to spend a night and a morning with her, Alex had a spike of cramp and caffeine deficiency. He was fading at the wheel in the mid-morning heat, so opened the windows wide and turned the radio up, just like a holidaying yob. He sought out a sign for a services stop.

It looked familiar. He had surely been in all of them between the two hubs of his life. It was emptying out – a school trip, he thought, disorganising itself back onto its bus. He stood in the small queue outwardly patient, but madly hungry, thirsty and in sore need of that caffeine. As he idled, he found himself looking for an empty table. He fixed on one occupied by two men, one older, one younger.

It was absurd, but from behind, under the stark restaurant lighting, designed to annoy people subtly and make them get out as quickly as they could, the younger man looked disturbingly like Nuria Hidalgo. Absurd – of *course*. Perhaps the lights were meant to give punters uncomfortable hallucinations too, just to make double-sure they would not linger. Alex was mesmerised. He gave his order on autopilot, watched his hands place his purchases onto his tray as if none of it belonged to him, reached absently into a pocket to pay and wandered off without his change. Laden with his food and drink, he sat at the table next to the two men. With no attempt to hide his interest, he examined the younger man's profile.

He took it to a point from which none of them could return without acknowledgement. The old man looked around at him and frowned. He nodded in reply to Alex's neutral greeting and his observation that the rain was never going to fall.

The younger man looked frankly at the interloper, a hint of amused familiarity under his ungainly fringe. The old man was a professional-looking fellow in his late fifties, perhaps, greying, balding, dressed somewhat stuffily – suit trousers and formal white shirt, sensible shoes with thin soles. The young man was painfully skinny – of course – bedenimmed, a hoodie loose on his bony shoulders and around his delicate wrists, his stiff black hair neither short nor long, and razored carelessly to somewhere in between. There was a hint of bravado in the amusement, half of his glance warily on the older man.

Alex caught a strange expression on the old fellow's face – puzzlement, Alex thought, at the idea of escorting this exotic creature. Maybe the man charged with bringing the first tiger to Europe had looked the same.

It would have been absurd for Alex to address the younger man as Nuria. Alex was afraid of his curiosity. He looked down at his food. He apologised, and said carefully that he had mistaken both of them for other people, citing that lack of caffeine, the low lighting, his contact lenses at the end of their month, many days of tiredness mounting up – that was how everyday his Spanish had become: good enough to gabble mad excuses.

He got up, left most of his food but brought his coffee with him and sat at another table, his back to the two men. Later, he put himself in the young man's position: young Alex Dante would have freaked out if a stranger had approached calling him, for example, Alexandra. And even kindly Jeffrey Dante would almost certainly have chinned the interloper. It *was* Nuria, though, it *was*; it *was* the exotic being once known as *Nuria Hidalgo* for sure, playing some kind of weird fucking game – as ever – but her, certainly a version of her: no other creature on earth could look *that* much like Nuria Hidalgo.

Alex noted movement, the clatter and clearing of trays, the gathering of stuff, the motions of leaving. There was a woman insisting on something unreasonable at the counter and knowing it, and making it worse by constantly laughing in short bursts, hoping that would make it better – it was a familiar annoyance to caterers. There was also a child with an irritating, piping voice in the background. Alex had to get out of there. He turned and looked towards the exit. Outside, the older man had gone into the toilets. The younger man waited. He toyed with a smile as Alex approached him.

"It's you," Alex said.

The boy unleashed Nuria's smile – *that* could be neither altered nor hidden.

"So," Alex began. The question could hardly be avoided. "Were you... always?"

"Always?" The narrowed eyes were mischievous.

"Yeah – you know, or did you..."

"What?" A young man thoroughly enjoying himself.

"*Change?*"

"Change?" He made a playful hiss that stopped just short of scorn, and laughed, but he kept a careful eye out for the return of the old man. "Well, maybe."

"Maybe?" Alex tried to laugh too, and nearly managed it.

"We all change, eh, Alexander?"

"*Alexander...*" It was Alex's turn to hiss and giggle.

"But listen."

"I'm listening."

There was the noise of a hand-dryer ebbing, an inner door opening and then the old man was with them once again. He took a long look at Alex and shared it with his companion; there was an opportunity there for any of them to speak, but only silence prevailed. The old man waited ten seconds, then opened the outer door and walked towards the car park, the young man following, gangly, awkward, but very, *very* sure of himself and of who he was.

Acknowledgements

Enormous thanks to my wife Jacqueline for her keen editor's eye and never-ending support.

Thanks also due to Paul Lyons, my eagle-eyed fellow-traveller. Thanks and gratitude to Diane Narraway and Julia Krzyzanowska and everybody at Veneficia for their faith in this book.

Long may it squiggle!

Other titles by Nick Sweeney:

Laikonik Express – Unthank Books, 2011

The Exploding Elephant – Bards and Sages, 2018

A Blue Coast Mystery, Almost Solved – Histria Books, 2020

The Émigré Engineer – Emerson College Ploughshares, 2021

Cleopatra's Script – Golden Storyline Books, 2022

The Fortune Teller's Factotum – Hear Our Voice Books, 2023